DRIFTWOOD

An Unspoiled Heiress Incognito

D. Iona Williams

DRIFTWOOD - AN UNSPOILED HEIRESS INCOGNITO

First Edition

Library of Congress Number 99-93730

Printed and bound in U.S.A. by
Tri-State Litho
71-81 Tenbroeck Ave.
Kingston, New York

For information, contact:
WILLIAMS BOOKS
999 5th Street S. E.
Winter Haven, FL 33880

This book is dedicated to two very special people.

First, to my mother, Miss T (as she is affectionately called), who taught me to pronounce those wonderful funny sounding words and corrected me until the hunger for knowledge, which I possessed even at that tender age of seven, abated.

Second, to my lovely daughter, Lauren, without whose encouragement and honesty I could not have accomplished this. Thank you for being such a friend and confidante, as well as for being you.

I love you both very much.

Pat
Thank you for your patronage
Hope you like it

This is a story of love and innocence,
romance and intrigue —
spanning more than two continents
and two generations.

Chapter One

The plane landed at the Montego Bay Airport, and Vivi's heartbeat sounded like thunder in her ears. What would she say to Ben when she finally met him? After all, up until then she had only seen pictures of him and spoken to him by telephone. But the sound of his voice still echoed in her head.

Meanwhile, the flight attendant was saying, "Welcome to Jamaica. We hope you have a pleasant stay, and thanks for flying Air Jamaica."

As Vivi's thoughts raced on, she went through the formalities of clearing customs and haltingly headed for the exit. Would she recognize him, she wondered, but more than that, would she like him?

There was the usual hustle and bustle in the waiting area as families and friends greeted each other, and Vivi wondered for the thousandth time why all the airports through which she traveled were crowded. The skycap brought out her luggage and she tipped him generously, while her eyes searched for the one face she might be able to distinguish among the hundreds.

Suddenly, there he was – much thinner than she had expected and also more handsome, she noticed, as he turned and looked in her direction. She watched him as he walked toward her and said, "Miss McNeil?"

"Yes. Mr. DeVille?"

"Welcome to Jamaica," he said, and picked up her luggage.

As she followed him to the waiting car, she smiled as she realized that she could love him, but she would wait.

Her thoughts were interrupted when he said, "Miss McNeil, do you mind sitting with the driver in order to make room for your bags?"

"Oh no!" she said. "That will be fine with me, but when are you going to begin calling me Vivi?"

He smiled and said, "I'm sorry. I guess I was waiting for your permission."

Until that moment, the only disappointment she had had was the fact that it was a rainy day; and that being temporary, was easily overlooked. But there was a certain reticence about Ben that she found both intriguing and disenchanting. She decided to forget about him for the moment, and soon began to enjoy the beautiful scenery of the countryside.

There were flowers of all colors, most of which she had never seen before, and they glistened like diamonds as the raindrops fell on them. Meanwhile, the car radio played, and something within her began to stir as she listened to the pulsating sound of "Reggae" music. She felt as if she was being drawn into a new experience as the music throbbed and she felt Ben's eyes as he watched her from behind.

Suddenly, wanting to break the spell, she said, "I never dreamed it could be so beautiful here."

"Oh!" said Ben. "Did I forget to mention in my letters how wonderful this place is?"

"Of course not. But I thought you were only trying to get me to visit."

The car sped around another corner, and Vivi tensed as she glanced at the precipice below, refusing to think what their fate would be should the driver miss a turn.

"Ross," Ben called to the driver, "please stop at the Gem. I think we could all use a drink."

Vivi was crushed. She expected him to ask her whether she wanted to stop, instead of assuming, but she said nothing.

They had passed through the dense woods and were driving along the seacoast where the road seemed to festoon the ocean's edge. And as she sat in mute fascination, she saw a sign, "Welcome to Hanover." This is it, she thought.

The car stopped, and Ben opened the door for her and took her hand. "I'm sorry if I seemed a bit distant, but I was so shocked at seeing you looking like that, I guess I got a little scared."

"Scared?" she said, walking with him to the bar. "I'm the one who's supposed to be scared. I have traveled halfway across the world to see you. I'm the one taking the chances."

"You're right, and I think I'll always love you for trusting me, but also I think I will explain when the time is right. There are some things I would like to tell you before anyone else does."

Vivi didn't understand what could cause such sadness in Ben, but she was aware of it, and although she was sure she wasn't the cause, it was quite evident it would affect her in some way.

She glanced at him, and his lips made her wonder what it would be like to be kissed by him. But she scolded herself for having such dark thoughts and again turned her attention to her surroundings, focusing on the waves as they splashed against the rocks below.

"Vivi," Ben said, "I know you have made reservations at the hotel, but I still think you would be better off in my home. Can I change your mind?"

"Thanks, Ben, but when I make decisions, I like to stick with them, unless there's cause for change, and right now I can't see any. Oh, bitter lemon on ice," she said. "This has always been my favorite drink, especially in hot weather."

They pulled up in front of an old building and Vivi read aloud "Driftwood Hotel." The disappointment was visible on her face, and Ben felt his plan was working fine as he said, "Now, are you sure you want to stay in this dingy place?"

"Ben DeVille," she said through half-clenched teeth, "I do not wish to stay in your home because I do not know your lifestyle, and I have no intention of being branded as one of your mistresses. I also do not want to be obligated to you in any other way, except maybe I will let you show me the island."

They both laughed, and he took her hand. "Vivi, please reconsider. It's not too late. . . . Don't you trust me?"

She retrieved her hand. "Of course I trust you," she said. "It is myself I'm afraid of. What if I attack you in the night?"

She laughed, and again Ben was tickled as well as fascinated by her accent. "You attacking me in my home?

Aren't you forgetting that I know all the secret passages? I would escape easily."

"From me or to me?" she said.

Gazing deep in her eyes, he said, "Vivi, that depends on you."

She was more than a little unnerved by his closeness, but she said, "I'll be fine, Ben." She picked up a bag and walked into the lobby toward the desk clerk.

***

The furnishings were new and the room was clean, but it lacked everything else. There were two single beds, a dressing table, and a chair, and Ben could tell that she was just putting up a brave front by staying there, but he could see by then how stubborn she was and knew he should respect her wishes. He could have put her in a fine place, but he thought when she saw the Driftwood, she would change her mind and stay with him.

"This is okay," she lied, as she stared out the window, where she had a perfect view of the ocean. And Ben knew that she deserved more, and was accustomed to better surroundings, but there was nothing he could do but wait.

Her next words caught him completely off guard when she said, "Ben, I'm starved. Do you know what time they serve dinner?"

Amazed at her ability to change moods, he said, "I don't know too much about this place, but while I inquire, how about having a drink with me?"

"That would be nice, thank you," she said.

Ben left he room and Vivi sighed heavily as she remembered her room at the DeVille's, her homes in New

York, and the thousand other places she might have been, but she chose the Driftwood. Instinctively she knew Ben allowed her to choose it with the hope she would refuse it; then he could take her home.

But two can play the game better than one, she told herself.

There was a knock on the door. "Come in." she called.

"Good evening, my lady!" said the plump little woman as she stood in the open doorway. "I'm Mrs Ashton. Mr. DeVille told me you were his friend, and I wanted to welcome you personally to my humble place. He's a fine gentleman, and any friend of his is surely welcome here. Dinner will be served in about half an hour, and remember to ask for anything you need. I will see to it personally. I do appreciate having a nice lady like yourself staying with us."

"Thank you, Mrs. Ashton, and I promise if I have any problems, you will be the first to know."

Ben walked in and sat on one of the beds. "Dinner is on its way up," he said. "But I have to ask you a question. Would you like to go out with me tonight?"

"Ben, I'm so tired, but where did you have in mind?"

"Well, there's this place I would like to show you, but if you can't make it tonight, there will be other times. Also, I have taken the liberty of ordering dinner for two. Do you mind?"

"Of course not," she replied with a stifled yawn, then got up and went to the bathroom, where she changed into a blue silk kimono. She went back into the room, threw herself across the bed quite unceremoniously and fell asleep almost immediately.

She had no idea how much time had passed, but when she again opened her eyes, Ben was standing over her with a very strange expression on his face. Too late she realized she was half exposed and tried to cover herself, but Ben was laughing.

She was furious.

"Vivi, you have such a beautiful body. Why are you so intent on hiding it?"

"Ben," she yelled, "I'm not accustomed to being spied on. You have no right coming in here unannounced." She forgot he was already there.

"But, my dear, you were sleeping, and I thought when you agreed to come here, it was in order for us to know each other better."

"Yes," she said, "but you cheated, and from now on, I'm going to keep a lock on the door."

"Even when we're married?"

"Don't be ridiculous, Ben. Whatever we said by pen and paper were just wasted emotions. What makes you think you can hold me to any of it? And furthermore, your reaction to my arrival here was not one of an enamored lover."

"I must warn you, Vivi, I hurt easily and I do not appreciate your choice of words, but if you could imagine what you mean to me, you wouldn't say those things. And as for me not loving you enough, that is impossible. I am still trying to assimilate the fact that you are here and that you came to me. If I have done anything to cause you to think otherwise, please forgive me."

She smiled, and he felt relieved, but he also detected a hint of mischief in her eyes.

"Ben," she said, "have I really slept through dinner?"

"No, my love, it's on its way up at this very moment."

"Didn't you say that already?"

Vivi soon forgot all her apprehension as she watched Ben open and pour the champagne, first giving her one glass and then taking the other, still holding her gaze. "To us," he said.

"Sorry, Ben, but I don't drink."

The shock on his face caused Vivi such delight. She said, "Didn't your teacher tell you not to assume anything?"

"Yes," Ben said. "As a matter of fact, he did. And I'm truly sorry. From now on, I'll ask you to tell me your will and pleasure."

When the tender moment faded, she felt flushed, and began to pick at the meal, but that soon passed and she began to eat with total abandon. Ben stared at her constantly, but refused to interrupt her obvious pleasure. But knowing he was watching her, she said, "Ben, when I leave here, I hope you won't remember me by the amount of food I eat."

"What amount?" said Ben.

"Oh!" she said in mock annoyance. "I have just eaten four lobsters."

They were both laughing now as Ben said, "Actually, that was two small lobsters split down the middle, and I'm glad you enjoyed it."

"How silly of me," she said.

"You, silly?" he said. "I'm the one who insists on making an ass out of you and myself." They both laughed again.

Not wanting to spoil her mood, Ben said, "We shouldn't keep you up any longer. Remember, you promised to let me take you out tonight."

"Oh, yes," she said. "I will try to be up and ready.

Ben DeVille was nobody's fool where women were concerned, but in Vivi he knew he had found an enigma. Her ability to change moods was fascinating to him as well as threatening, yet he wanted her as he had never wanted anyone before. He smiled at her and said, "Shall I pick you up about eleven thirty? There will be a live show at midnight."

"As you wish, Monsieur," she said, saluting as they both got to their feet.

He headed toward the door and she followed him, but when he reached for her, she wordlessly opened the door and he stepped out.

Relief flooded her whole being as she leaned against the closed door, knowing instinctively that he was doing the same on the other side, and she stood there until she heard him move and his footsteps faded in the corridor. Sensing a bond between them but refusing to admit it even to herself, she hoped he didn't see through her act. She would much rather that he thought she was a little tired than for him to know the truth.

She was grateful there was no television in the room to distract her this time, and she began to sum up what she knew about Ben as she chose something to wear. But she soon realized how futile her effort was to discredit him, and turned to the only other source of relief she knew. She had a shower and went to bed.

She was awakened by a knock on the door, and she struggled to adjust her mind to her surroundings as she blinked, as if that would change things, but they remained. Then she remembered. "Ben, Ben!" she called. "Do come in."

The knob turned, but he didn't come in. Then she realized it was locked. "Oh Ben!" she said sleepily, "I'm so sorry. Were you here long?"

"Not really. I fell asleep, and it wasn't until Ross came to pick me up that I got up. I don't know what I'd do without him."

Ben's remark did not go unnoticed by Vivi, but she withheld her comment and concentrated on getting dressed. As she reappeared in blue jeans that fitted her perfectly, Ben found it difficult not to stare at her, and he was proud of having her for his date. "I'm sure I'll be the envy of all the men at Roxy's tonight," he said. "You look fantastic."

***

The Roxy was one of the most uniquely structured buildings Vivi had ever seen, with its high ceiling and low couches, a circular bar in its center and fruits of all descriptions hanging from the beams. On one side was a music room from which emitted the soothing sound of Reggae, to which she was becoming quite accustomed. Never did she expect to find such a place in the Caribbean. The lighting was like home, she thought, and immediately regretted the memory when Ben said, "Do you mind looking around before we're seated?"

"Of course not. I think it's wonderful here. If only for this, I'm glad I came."

Ben was tickled, but said nothing. Instead, he went to the bar and ordered their drinks. They went out in the cool night air and sat beneath almond trees with tables and chairs built around them. They wandered down paths to the ocean and the pool as the winsome fragrance of wild flowers winnowed through the evening breeze. When Ben took her hand, she didn't resist, but proceeded to ask him inconsequential questions to prolong the moment. "Oh, Ben," she finally said, "it's intoxicating."

"Yes," he said, determined not to change her mood. He wanted her to be the way she was for the rest of their lives together, but he dared not say it until the time was right.

"Who built this place?" she asked,

"Well," he said, "if rumors are to be believed, it was built by a Russian defector who was picked up and returned before it was completed."

"I'm glad he didn't have the chance to complete it, or I might have hated it then," she said with a spark of mischief in her eyes.

Wordlessly, Ben took her free hand and kissed it, then led the way back inside. He seldom took his eyes off her as she watched in muted fascination as the natives danced to the pulsating rhythm of Reggae.

On becoming aware of his presence, she smiled at him and he held out his hand and said, "Shall we?"

"Oh, no!" she answered hastily.

"Why not?" he said.

"Well," she said, "there's something you should know, but you must promise not to repeat it to a single soul."

Ben became slightly alarmed and said, "Your secret is safe with me, Vivi, but if it will jeopardize our relationship in any way, you don't have to tell me."

"But I want to tell you," she insisted, "although it is quite difficult for me to admit."

Ben was staring at her with such concern in his eyes she couldn't stand it anymore. "Ben," she said, "I have two left feet."

"Oh, my God!" he said. "How could such a terrible thing happen to a wonderful creature like you?"

Their laughter could be heard around the room, but they were oblivious to everything but each other, and when he kissed her, she felt a surge of electricity through their contact that she had never experienced before.

"Vivi," he said, "I've waited all my life for you."

She knew she should resist him, but she allowed the sweet flow to course through her body, and soon all her carefully erected barriers began to crumble. The moment might have passed but for the DJ's rendition of "Your Precious Love" by Percy Sledge, which seemed to say all the things they so desperately needed to say but were either afraid or unable to. Willingly, she lost herself in his arms on the dance floor, not caring how long they danced as long as that feeling remained with her always.

When they finally sat down again, Ben said, "Vivi, for some unexplained reason, I've tried to find the meaning of your name, and the more I tried the more fascinated I became. But the closest I've come to a meaning is the word 'life.' Well, you have given me life in a very special way, and I want to make you my life, if you let me."

She began to protest, but heard herself say instead, "There's no need for any promises, Ben. I thank you for inviting me here, and whatever I've seen so far already surpasses my expectations. I truly think I'm going to like it here. It all seems so beautiful."

"And so are you, Vivi."

She felt the flush in her cheeks, and was suddenly grateful for the dimness of the light, but she couldn't miss the admiration in his voice when he said, "You're a good fighter, Vivi, but may the best man win."

Ben had introduced her to Campari, and not being accustomed to such things, she was sure that her feelings were all on account of the drink. Not wanting to admit her true feelings, she refused the next drink, saying she had had enough.

"Vivi," Ben said, "what are you afraid of?"

"Afraid?" she said. "Why should I be? Are you saying you're dangerous to be with?"

"No, but you sure act like it. One moment you're happy and outgoing, and the next you seem to retreat into a shell."

Now there were sparks in her eyes, and Ben could hear the annoyance in her voice as she said, "I think it's time you took me home. You have succeeded in ruining a beautiful evening, Mr DeVille."

"I'm sorry, Vivi," said Ben. "After all the fun we've shared, I cannot let you leave angry with me. Forgive me, but all I'm trying to do is to get to know you. You know as well as I that if you didn't believe there was the slightest possibility that you could care for me, you wouldn't have come all this way."

"Yes," she said, "you are right, but for tonight can't we just forget about that?"

"Okay, I have the perfect thing for you. Wait here." He returned with two cups of conch soup laced with hot pepper, and before long they were talking again, and Vivi began to relax.

They talked at length about the music and its origins, and Vivi tried desperately to describe the feeling it gave her.

"You are a perfect convert, my dear," said Ben, "because people do say the music has to be felt, not explained."

He was grateful for the truce and promised himself not to upset her again that night, but he had no intention of giving up until he reached his goal. With her guard down, she looked so vulnerable and even younger than she was, and Ben vowed to protect her from as many hurts as possible, although he couldn't tell her so.

"Vivi," he said, "I promised Ross I'd pick him up at his friend's club; do you mind if we leave now? We could come back after we take him home."

"That won't be necessary, Ben. I've already overstayed. It's been a long time since I was out this late."

She waited for him at the entrance while he brought the car around, and there it was: a tree completely covered by a parasitic vine, which she recognized as a member of the philodendron family. It seemed cut to form as it claimed the life of the tree which was now only visible by portions of the trunk.

Ben drove up and saw her lost in thought. "Isn't that beautiful?" she said. "I would like to get a picture of it — such cruel, quiet beauty, it's simply breathtaking. I shall never forget this place or this night!" she said.

"Neither shall I, Vivi, which proves we have something in common after all."

When the car took off, she yelled, "Are you crazy? How can you speed on a road like this?"

"I'm used to it," he yelled back, "and I'm late."

"You are also a wretched driver," she said.

"I'll admit I am if you admit you are enjoying every minute of it."

She didn't reply, but from the expression on her face, he knew he was right.

They drove for about five minutes more when he suddenly stopped in a crowd of people. Vivi froze as she gazed at what must have been hundreds of young men with their hair all rolled up and falling around their faces. To her they looked menacing, but Ben simply laughed and said, "They are Rastifarians. They won't hurt you."

Out of fear, Vivi clung to Ben's arm, and soon they entered a hall where the music blared while the people stood around listening. Pushing through the crowd, they finally reached a kind of podium. Ben stopped and whispered in her ear, "Wait here," and before she had a chance to protest, he was gone.

All she could do was stand there and wait for whatever was going to happen to her, but Ben reappeared and her heart stopped racing. As he led her toward the door, the people started to cheer, and Vivi, feeling she had missed something, said, "What was that all about?"

"I'm not sure," Ben said, "but a lot of them work for me, and I guess they approve of their new mistress."

"Ben DeVille!" she said. "You are the most conceited man I've met so far, and I hope there's none like you in my future."

"There's no need to worry about your future, my love. I shall see that you never even speak to another man."

He was baiting her, and she knew it. "Ben," she said, "I am truly disappointed in you. I never thought you were capable of male chauvinism."

"Vivi, why should I lack such a gentlemanly quality? What would you think of me then? That I'm a pussycat?"

She liked his sense of humor, and was surprised at the ease with which he spoke. It was all so contagious.

Ross appeared and they changed the subject, but Vivi knew that her resolve to make it a vacation and nothing else was severely threatened. She began to think of Ben being with other women in a similar situation, and was amazed at her reaction. She was glad they had reached her hotel, and as she hurried up to her room, Ben noticed the change in her, but had no idea what brought it on.

"Would you like me to stay with you tonight, Vivi?"

"Oh no! I'm fine."

He kissed her cheek and said, "Can't blame a man for trying, can you?"

"Bye, Ben," she said. "See you later, and I mean much later."

While undressing, Vivi tried to remember everything that had happened that night, and when she fell asleep, she had a satisfied smile on her face.

Chapter Two

Her two-week stay became three, and whenever she mentioned leaving, Ben convinced her to stay. They went everywhere that was worth seeing, and Vivi loved being with him, although at times one would never know it. She was given to lapses of sadness like Ben, and he wondered if her reasons were half as serious as his.

She ate foods she never knew existed, and even went to the races in Spanish Town, where she was featured in the fashion column of the next day's *Gleaner.* She was so excited. "But how do they know who I am?" she asked.

"Well," Ben said, "they asked my permission, and I said it was okay as long as they kept it simple."

Mr. Watts knew and respected Ben. All he said was that the dress was worn by the beautiful Miss McNeil, a visitor to the island. Vivi was secretly pleased but said, "Ben DeVille, one of these days I'm going to repay you for the things you do to me."

"Oh Miss McNeil, I'm looking forward to that more than you will ever know."

She threw an orange at him, and he caught it as if he anticipated her every move. It was time to stop resisting Ben, at least mentally, but she refused to let her emotions take the same course. There were still some unexplained doubts in her mind concerning his professed love for her, even though she finally admitted to herself that she was hopelessly in love with him. She decided it was time to tell him of her past, such as it was, and provide for him the opportunity to do the same.

Determined to get it over with, she said, "Let's have a picnic tomorrow, Ben."

"Sure!" he said. "Where do you have in mind?"

"Well," she said, "seeing you're the brain, why don't you select the site while I choose the menu."

"No!" he said. "Tell you what, I will choose the site and you can select the menu. How's that?"

"Ben, you are trying to drive me crazy, but I won't let you." She had never laughed so much in her whole life.

Ben's easy banter was new to her, and she was deep in thought when he said, "If you are having trouble with me choosing the spot for the picnic, why don't you do it? You should know I would go anywhere with you."

"Ben," she said, "have you ever been serious about anything?"

"Yes," he said, gazing into her eyes, "but on the other hand, I would hate to go on a serious picnic."

He kissed her as she opened her mouth in total disbelief, but he could see that she loved every minute of it.

The estate was large, and the following morning they started out early in order to cover enough ground before the sun came up. Vivi rode a different horse from the stables on Ben's advice. "This one is accustomed to long distances," he said.

They traveled along a path for several miles, then they went into the undergrowth at the edge of the forest. "Ben,"

Vivi yelled as the horse trotted along, "are you telling me you own all this land?"

"The last I checked, I had five hundred acres on this side, so this is really a part of it."

"Are you sure you have a particular place in mind, or are we just wandering aimlessly?" she said, changing the subject.

"There is an old shack up ahead where the men sometimes stay when they work in this area. We should be there soon."

Within minutes she was able to see the open shack beyond a stream. Immediately Vivi noticed the deep blue of the water and said, "How is it that the water looks like the ocean?"

Ben told her the stories of mermaid sightings, and her fascination grew as he related the many versions.

"When I write my memoirs, I shall include the day at 'little sea' with my lover."

"Vivi, aren't you a little ahead of things? First, I'm not your lover, and second, you have no idea what this day has in store for you."

"Right again," she said. "But would you mind if we sat under the tree instead of in there?"

"As you wish, madame. You know I'm incapable of saying no to you."

They dismounted, and Vivi looked around for the perfect spot. When she found it, she proceeded to spread the blankets. The basket, which looked awfully heavy to her, contained a large variety of fresh fruits, some of which Vivi had grown to love, including pineapple slices and mangoes. Also there was chicken, fish, bread, cheese, and several containers of sodas and juices.

"Ben!" said Vivi. "Why so much? Aren't we going home tonight?"

"Of course we are. But when Annie packs lunch, that's how it is."

They ate and talked and ate some more while Vivi told him of the highlights of her childhood. He talked about his parents and school, then his inheritance, his hobbies, and most of the things she had already known.

To change the mood, she said, "I'd like to wash up a bit. Let's go to the stream."

Ben agreed and started to run down the incline with her in tow. Breathing heavily she said, "You know, I've never done anything like this before."

"Why?" he said.

"Because I've spent the greater part of my life in school, and I've never known anyone like you."

"Sorry you missed so much," said Ben, "but you still have time to catch up. My only hope is that you will let me teach you all the things you need to know."

"Thanks for the offer, but at times I doubt my own feelings, and I wouldn't want to do anything that either of us would regret."

"Vivi, I love you! I've never wanted another woman since I saw your picture."

This time she held his gaze and said, "How do I know that there isn't some deep, dark secret you are trying to hide while you speak so passionately of your love for me?"

"Our love, Vivi, is all that matters to me. Whatever may or may not have happened in the past, is just past."

The caress of the light breeze on her face made her more relaxed. She rested her chin in her hand and looked up at Ben. "At times I believe you," she said, "but in my mind there are still questions to be answered, and until they are, I can't make a de —"

There was a sudden thud between them and Vivi froze, then started to scream As her fear grew, so did her screams until her mouth opened but there was no sound.

"Don't move!" ordered Ben. "If you do, it might run toward you, but it's harmless. It's just as frightened as you are." Then with one swift motion, he pulled the blanket and threw the iguana away.

Vivi still did not move, and Ben, realizing she was in shock, picked her up and placed her on her horse, hoping she would feel safe there. He noticed she was trembling and she still hadn't spoken. He took one of the containers from the basket and tried to make her drink, but she gagged instead.

"It's okay, Vivi! You don't have to be afraid. It can't hurt you. Please say something."

She just sat there, eyes trained on the blanket in which the reptile was trapped. The day was ruined; the only thing to do was to take her home. If only she would say something. Her body was as rigid as if frozen into position. He went for his horse, wondering what to do, when without warning her horse started at a gallop.

"Oh my God!" he yelled. "Vivi, hold on! Hold on!" Ben caught his mount and started after her, but that made her horse go faster. Relief flooded his mind when she started toward the stream. Maybe she only wanted a drink. But he soon discovered the horse had no intention of stopping. She jumped in an attempt to cross it, and Vivi was thrown to the other side. "Please, God!" he prayed, "don't let her be hurt," he said as he approached her still form.

He cradled her head in his arms, but she didn't stir. "Vivi!" he called while he wiped the dirt from her face, but there was no answer. He laid her down gently and removed his shirt and soaked it in the stream, then squeezed the water on her face with as much force as possible. She groaned.

There was a lump on the side of her head, but she slowly opened her eyes, and Ben's heart was flooded with relief. "Thank God!" he said. "You're okay. But don't try to talk. I must get you to the doctor."

"What happened?" she whispered.

"You were thrown by that miserable animal you were riding, but there's no need to talk about that now. I'm going to pick you up."

"Ben, my ankle hurts. I think it's broken."

"I hope not, but let me look at it."

As he tried to remove her boot, she cried out and gripped his arm.

"Darling, he said, "I don't mean to alarm you, but if I don't do this now, it will hurt even more later."

Through her protests, he removed it and discovered that the ankle was beginning to swell.

The pain in Vivi's ankle intensified, but so did her desire for the man who held her close as they rode together silently, each with their own thoughts. Feeling a bit foolish, she broke the silence. "Oh Ben, I feel like a fool, and you must think I'm a baby, but I'm terrified of those things."

She shivered at the memory, and Ben tightened his hold on her waist reassuringly, hoping to allay her fears. He said, "I promise there will be no more iguanas if you promise that I will always be able to hold you like this."

Still resisting him outwardly, she said, "Ben DeVille!" in the meanest tone she could muster. "The only promise I will ever make to you is that one day I'm going to get you for all the things you've done to me."

Ignoring her feigned temper, he said, "Believe me, my love, that's good enough for me."

Dr. Grey's office was crowded, but when Ben DeVille entered with Vivi in his arms, they were shown to a room and the nurse told him the doctor would see him right away. By then, Vivi's ankle was badly swollen and her head throbbed from the lump she had received from the fall, but her mind was functioning enough to notice the special treatment that was always accorded to Ben by everyone.

Soon the doctor entered the room. "What have we here, Ben?" he said cheerfully.

"Well, Doc, this is Miss McNeil. We went riding and she was thrown by her horse."

Dr. Grey stared at Vivi as he reached for her hand. "My pleasure, Miss, but I think. . . . Oh! Forgive me," he continued. "Ben, I think I'll give her a thorough examination to make sure there is nothing wrong except her ankle. Please wait outside and let the nurse come in."

Ben smiled as he thought of the old Doc's reaction to Vivi. It had happened to a lot of people, but somehow there seemed to be more in the almost sad eyes of this man.

Meanwhile, Dr. Grey was saying, "Miss McNeil, I'm sorry if I offended you by staring, but I thought I recognized you. Then I soon realized I was wrong. You will forgive an old man, won't you?"

"Sure, Doctor. Just as soon as I get rid of the pain in my ankle and my head, that will be my next task," she said, visibly annoyed.

"Well, lucky lady, from what I've seen, there are no broken bones, but you are a bit banged up. I suggest you take it easy for a while. The nurse will take care of you and I'll give you a prescription for painkillers. I would like to see you a week from today to check that ankle, but if you have any problems before, please don't hesitate to call me."

"Thank you, Doctor."

Tired of waiting outside, Ben came in somewhat hesitantly. "How is she, Doc?"

"She's fine, Ben. It's a sprain, but you know those things are a bit tricky. You have to keep her off her feet as much as possible. But then, with your reputation, that shouldn't be difficult."

"Look, Doc, she's not just any woman."

"I can see that, Ben, but does she remind you of anyone?"

"I'm glad you mentioned that, Doc. I thought it was just me. I never really believed in reincarnation, but if there's really such a thing, would it be decent for me to marry her? Please believe me, Doc, she has changed my whole life. I'm not able to feel anything for another woman, and it scares me."

"Pull yourself together, Ben. Where was she born?"

"In the United States."

"Well, think of it as coincidental and consider yourself lucky. Although I must admit, the resemblance is uncanny. My God, man, I envy you."

Just then the nurse came in, with Vivi leaning against her. Ben shook hands with Dr. Grey and promised to carry out his instructions, saying, "After all, her accident was my fault."

Dr. Grey hurried to his next patient and apologized for staying so long, then continued to chatter away as if he had something to hide. He felt like a child would if he were caught in the proverbial cookie jar. How could he get this woman out of his mind? After so many years, he had finally forgotten her. Why did she have to come back to haunt him? Would he never be rid of her? It had to be an omen that she would return in the same family. But how could it be? "Oh my God!" he whispered. "Am I getting senile?"

Jeanette DeVille was the most beautiful woman he had ever seen, and for him it was love from that moment on. That was over twenty-five years ago, but she was with a man whom they said she lived with. How could she have done such a thing when he would have treated her like a queen?

He could still remember the way she looked at him years later, when he had finally gotten the nerve to tell her how he felt. "Is that a proposal?" she had said. "Well, Doctor, you're very kind, but I'm afraid it's too late. If I had time, I might even take you up on your offer, but I'm dying, Stephen." It was the first time she had called him by his first name.

He had held her close and she laid her head on his shoulder and cried. How long he had dreamed of holding her in his arms, and then he finally did, but she was dying. "Jeanette, my darling, cry if you must, but I think you are overreacting. I think I can help you to see things clearly. I'll give you a checkup and prove to you how wrong you are."

But she was right. She had an advanced stage of pulmonary tuberculosis. All his hopes and dreams that she might notice him came through and were shattered in one hour.

Five months later she died, and a part of him died with her. He was so broken up, he couldn't attend the funeral. Now here she was again, in another body maybe, with those eyes that had haunted him all these years.

***

As Vivi lumbered along on Ben's arm she knew what his next request was going to be, and was not surprised when he said, "Now I want you to move into my home. There will be people to look after you, and you will be more comfortable."

"I most certainly will not!" she protested. "Now that I'm disabled, I will need my privacy even more, and I don't want your pity."

"Vivi!" he said in obvious annoyance. "I do believe a woman of your intelligence can differentiate between genuine concern and pity. Furthermore, I'm convinced you're going to need somebody to help you, and you know it too."

Vivi was furious. "Ben DeVille," she said, "you are nothing but a big bully, but the answer is still no."

Ben could hear the fear in her voice, and wondered what could cause her to be so adamant about not staying in his home. He helped her up to her room in silence, and she hoped he wasn't angry with her, but she was afraid to find out.

Not being able to help herself, she said, "Would you like to stay for a while?"

"Oh no!" he said. "After the compliment you paid me a while ago, I'd rather not, but I'll send Annie to look in on you later."

He left, and she felt guilty for attacking him the way she did. What if she had hurt him so deeply that he never wanted to see her again?

She felt as if she was doing the right thing. She had to be sure before she told him. But then, there was the unmistakable bond between him and Ross which brought Rojea Molen and his chauffeur to mind. She knew she wasn't paranoid, and decided to keep things the way they were until she was certain.

Ben stayed away the rest of that day and did not show up for dinner as usual. When Mrs. Ashton sent a tray up for her much later, she tried to eat, but without Ben, she couldn't. She was in terrible pain, not only from her bruises, but she refused to admit it, even to herself.

She tried desperately to sleep, but sleep eluded her. In her confusion, she made a decision: she would catch the first flight she could and return home. The word "home" echoed in her head, and she was struck by the sudden realization that she had none.

There was no one anywhere waiting for her, only places, empty houses and things. There were no people. She was truly alone.

The tears streamed down her face as she began to pack, throwing things as hard as she could and not caring anymore about order. Suddenly there was a knock on the door, and she dragged herself over to open it. Ben was standing there, looking every bit as miserable as she felt. No one spoke. They met and held each other while she sought release in her tears.

Ben felt her body relax against his, and knew he was right about her. He took her face in both hands and said, "You love me, don't you?"

"Yes, I do love you but. . . ."

He kissed her, tenderly at first, then he became possessive, and she yielded to him as it penetrated her very being. With all the hidden desires she had suppressed through the years awakened, she clung to him, and laughed and cried alternately as relief swept over her. Her emotions freed at last, she giggled as Ben picked her up and spun her around saying, "Vivi, you've made me a happy man. But I could be happier. Say you'll marry me."

"Yes," she said, "I will marry you," and was immediately deliriously happy by just uttering the words.

"Now, darling, we've got to make plans. First the banns have to be announced, which takes at least three weeks, and I've got other things to do, so shall we say a month from today?"

Vivi watched him in quiet amusement as he became all businesslike. She said, "Shhh," touching her fingers to his lips. "Not so fast, Monsieur. We must be sensible about this. There are things I would have to do, as well as know, before I marry you."

"Well," he said, "I'm sorry if I seem eager, but I think we should get it over before you change your mind. You see, I can't imagine spending the rest of my life without you. After that little incident today, I realized how much you mean to me. I was so empty without you, and when I thought of losing you, it frightened me so I just had to do the right thing."

"Well, Mr. DeVille, if confession is truly good for the soul, let me purge myself by telling you how miserable I felt for those few hours. Suddenly it dawned on me I was lonely. I thought the only thing to do was go home, but soon remembered that there was no one to welcome me back in the way that it would have mattered. In that brief moment, I became aware that all I had was you. I thank you for saving me from making a mistake I would regret the rest of my life."

***

Vivi's recovery was quick, due partly to her state of mind but mostly to the attention she got from Ben and his housekeeper, Annie. Although she continued to live at the hotel, they catered to her every whim, and within the month she was well enough to travel. But wanting everything to be perfect, she stayed on until her limp was completely gone.

Chapter Three

Saying goodbye to Ben was more difficult than she thought, but there was no other way. She had to make sure her affairs were in order, and she had to make a will. As morbid as the idea seemed, it was necessary, and she knew it.

That weekend in her Fifth Avenue apartment, everything looked dreary and insignificant to her. The beautiful furnishings which were once her parents' and all the things she had so cherished over the years had lost their meaning. Ben had become the focal point in her life, and now she was able to admit it there was no reason to deny it anymore. With no relatives, and her best friend in Paris, it was good to know that in Ben she could have it all.

She awoke early Monday morning and the thought of what she was about to do was exhilarating. She had finally grown up and was about to take charge of her life. Ignoring the twinge of guilt she felt for not telling Ben about her financial status, convincing herself that he could only be pleasantly surprised, she made some instant coffee and showered leisurely, then chose a winter white wool suit from her wardrobe.

She looked exquisite, thanks to the few pounds she had gained on her vacation, and she felt good, thinking of the new life she was going to have with Ben. She made sure her accessories were matching perfectly, and even regretted having to wear a coat, but after all, it was only March.

Downstairs, Max the doorman said, "Hello, Miss McNeil. It's good to see you, ma'am."

"Thanks, Max. It's always nice to come back to New York. Will you get me a taxi, please?"

"Right away, ma'am." Noticing the change in her, but not daring to question her, he only hoped it was a good man she found, because his well trained eyes told him she had the look of love in hers.

Her father had been very kind to him, and after his death, she came back but seldom stayed there. He opened the door for her and she thanked him with a little grin. She was so lovely, he thought as she got in and drove off.

Vivi sat back and gave the driver the address on West Fifty-seventh Street. New York! she thought. It seemed she knew the three most wonderful places on earth, and fortunately she was able to call each of them home at one time or other. Like New York, she always felt good returning to Paris, and soon she would be living in Jamaica permanently.

While she mused, the taxi took her across town and she was now at her destination. She paid the driver and entered the building where she searched the directory and took the elevator to the fourth floor.

She began checking the numbers to the left, and soon came upon room four-fifteen. She pressed the buzzer, and the door opened as if they had expected someone. "I'm Vivi McNeil," she said. "I'm here to see Mr. Phipps."

The young woman at the desk looked at her in stunned silence, then after recovering said, "Do you have an appointment?"

"No, but I'm here to settle my estate. This is the office of Agar & Phipps, is it not?" she said to the stupefied woman.

"Oh, yes, Miss McNeil, but you see, Mr. Phipps passed away over a year ago, and there's only Miss Phipps here this early."

"Pardon my ignorance, miss, but I spend most of my time out of the country and was not aware of his passing."

Vivi was a bit annoyed at her for the way she stared, and picked up a magazine to ease her discomfort, but she only turned the pages. She was positive they had never met, but there was recognition in her eyes, and Vivi began to resent her boldness.

The firm of Agar & Phipps was established in eighteen ninety-eight and was now under the supervision of the third generation, but unfortunately, Oswald Phipps never had a son. He was thrilled when his wife Matilda announced that she was pregnant, but to his dismay, she gave birth to a girl and was unable to bear more children, due to ill health.

The baby grew a bit more quickly than was expected, and they became quite concerned, but their doctor assured them she was healthy and there was nothing he could do. She continued to grow, and her father knew if she continued at that pace, he would never get her married, but since she was bright, he did the only thing he could. He taught her everything he knew and treated her like the son he never had.

She spent most of her time studying law and passed the bar in record time, so that her towering height and masculine appearance ceased to worry her father. He knew his heart wouldn't hold out as long as he wished, but he wanted to leave his practice in capable hands. He had been proud of the outcome of his decision. She wasn't what he wanted, but she certainly would have to do.

In the years that followed, he watched her grow in knowledge and size, and when it was rumored that she was Van McNeil's mistress, his only reaction was, what did he see in her?

Oswald Phipps was a reasonable man, and he accepted the fact that there were not going to be any grandchildren to leave his fortune to, but just suppose there was even an illegitimate one! How unkind nature can be, he thought, and the pain in his chest intensified. Before he could be helped, he died, leaving his practice and all his worldly goods to his daughter, Phyllis.

"You may go in now, Miss McNeil," said the receptionist.

"Oh thank you!" Vivi said without looking at her.

"Hello, Miss Phipps," she said, extending a hand. "I'm Vivi McNeil."

The woman half-raised herself, and Vivi thought she was in the presence of a giant. "Do sit down," she said. "So we finally meet. Vivi, may I call you Vivi?"

"Of course."

"All these years I sent you your allowance, I wondered what you looked like, but I never dreamed you were so beautiful."

Vivi blushed. "Thank you," she said, "but I'm here to settle my estate. You see, there are a few changes I have to make."

There was a sudden change in the lawyer's countenance. "Are you complaining about the way I've handled your affairs after all these years?"

"Of course not. Daddy left enough in my account, and with my allowance I never needed anything, but now it's all going to be different. Miss Phipps, I'm going to be married."

"Married! Vivi, are you out of your mind?"

Vivi stared at her in total disbelief, and found herself completely at a loss for words.

"I'm so sorry, Vivi. Please forgive me. I forgot that you are grown now, but until you're twenty-one, as executrix, it is my obligation to see that you dispense with your holdings adequately."

"That is the reason I'm here, Miss Phipps. I want you to sell the property in New Rochelle and also make my future husband sole beneficiary to my estate until we have children."

"Well, if you insist, but I will have to have whatever information you can provide, in order to expedite the process. Vivi, how long have you known this man?"

"Long enough, I assure you. I would also like one hundred thousand dollars in my account so I can prepare for my wedding."

"Young lady!" screamed Phyllis as she removed what seemed like a man's handkerchief from her pocket and wiped her ample brow. "I think you're being foolish. And furthermore, it all depends on whether your request meets with our criteria."

"Miss Phipps, how dare you treat me like a beggar! Might I remind you that you are being paid handsomely for your services?"

"Yes, of course, I'm sorry. But your request is unusual, and I know your late father would want me to act in your best interest."

In that brief mention of her father's name, Vivi thought she saw a hint of femininity in Phyllis Phipps, but it was gone just as quickly as it came. Meanwhile, the pain was renewed in both their hearts – for Vivi, how she missed her father; and for Phyllis, how she ached for the only man who had ever touched her. There was the painful reminder that he only came to her when he was drunk, but he was all she had. There was no one else then, and maybe never again.

Awakening from her reverie, she saw Vivi stand up as if to leave, and she pulled herself up to her full height, reached out a hand and said, "Congratulations, Vivi. I wish you all the happiness you seek, and I will attend to your request personally."

Vivi walked out of the office of Agar & Phipps somewhat less elated than she should have been, for something about Phyllis was troubling her. Without meaning to, her mind wandered to a story she had read as a child, and with the form of Phyllis fresh in her mind, she said aloud, "Now I know how the poor Lilliputians must have felt."

Her mind returned to normal as she rushed out into the cold air and hailed a taxi. On reaching the apartment, she called the airline and made a reservation for the following day. Then she went to Bloomingdale's and picked up a few gifts. She had no friends in New York, so she spent most of her time in the stores. Then later, she called Marguerite and arranged for her to meet her at the airport.

Vivi knew she had made a major decision, but it wasn't a hasty one. She was truly in love with Ben and was looking forward to being his wife, but she missed having someone to share her happiness. Lying across her bed, she wished her father was alive, and she missed her nanny so much, but most of all, she missed her mother.

The way she felt, she would discuss her plans with almost anyone, even Tessie, her stepmother, but she, too, was gone. As her mind wandered, her eyes closed and she drifted off to sleep, where she dreamed she was with Ben running on the beach. When she awoke, she discovered it was only a dream, but all her love for him was renewed. She couldn't believe it was only four days since they said goodbye; she was so lonely without him.

In order to change her mood, she decided to pack for her trip, and as she busied herself, she started to think of all the things she had to do once she got there. At six o'clock the phone rang, and she knew it would be Ben.

"Hello my love!" he yelled in the receiver.

"I'm fine, darling. But why are you yelling?"

"I'm not. But tell me, how are things? Are we still getting married?"

"Ben! What made you think not?"

"Oh, honey, I miss you so at times, I wonder whether I did the right thing letting you go."

"Ben DeVille, you are even more crazy than I imagined. It is only four days since I left. What are you going to do for the next three months?"

"Three months! You never said anything about that before you left. And Vivi, why did you leave the money I gave you?"

"Because it wasn't necessary. I told you I would take care of myself. Don't worry, Ben, when I need it, you will be the first to know. Anyway, I am going to see Marguerite tomorrow to ask her to be my maid of honor. That should tell you I am thinking of getting married."

They talked for over an hour. Neither one wanted to say goodbye, but when they did, they were both certain that nothing could stop the love they felt for each other.

That night Ben was restless. There was something about Vivi he didn't know. Her independence seemed to be more than pride. Why didn't she accept any financial help from him? He was accustomed to giving gifts to women, and although Vivi was wonderfully different, or unlike anyone he had ever known, he wanted to be kind to her. Who really was Vivi McNeil?

He didn't have the answer to that, but he loved her, and whoever she turned out to be, he was going to marry her.

Meanwhile, Vivi was struggling with her conscience – whether she had done the right thing by not telling Ben she was wealthy. But she wanted him to marry her, not her money, and she was positive this time that what he didn't know couldn't hurt him. In the conversation they had just had, she told him that they didn't pay dowry anymore, but it was still the duty of the bride's parents to fund the wedding.

"But you have no parents, Vivi. Please let me help. And why do you have to go for Marguerite? Can't you just call her and tell her, then send her a letter with the details?"

"No, Ben. I need her to help me select my trousseau, and I have to see her parents."

He sounded a bit dissatisfied, but he didn't press her any further, and that was surely not a good time to tell him. Now she longed for the daylight when she would catch the plane to see Marguerite and tell her the good news, that she was going to marry her cousin Ben after all.

Before she left, she wanted to hear his voice once more, and she had also decided on a date for the wedding. She knew he would still be asleep, but she had to put his mind at ease, and when he picked up the phone, her heart skipped the usual beat at the sound of his voice.

"Hello, sleepy head."

"Vivi! What time is it? Why are you up so early?"

"One question at a time, please."

"Okay, love. Why are you up so early?"

"Because I'm leaving this morning, and I have something to tell you. I have decided on a date for our wedding."

"You have?"

"Yes. June twenty-first."

"Thank you, darling. Now I will never go back to sleep, but I want you to know I will always love you and I promise you won't regret it."

"I love you too, Ben, and I'll write you soon."

***

Marguerite was excited that Vivi was going to become a part of the family, but she was purely ecstatic when Vivi asked her to be her maid of honor. "Oh, *cherie*, I am so happy for you and my cousin Ben. Now I will be meeting him for the first time. It is all so romantic. But first, you must tell me all about Jamaica, and then we go shopping."

"Shopping! Marguerite, I have just flown thousands of miles. Don't you think I need to rest?"

"Oui, *cherie*, but it is the excitement. I cannot think. We will need to make a list so that we forget nothing. Are you going to buy furnishings?"

"No, that won't be necessary, but I will need vases, crystals from Lalique, and linen suitable for the climate. Also a king-size mosquito net. I will take the silverware and china that belonged to my parents, plus a few mementos, but I intend to keep the New York apartment so we can visit when we want to. Ben has a marvelous housekeeper who is very efficient, but when it becomes my home, I want it to be perfect. I'm only hoping that they all won't resent me, and that Ben, most of all, will be delighted in whatever changes I might make."

"Oh, *cherie*! When are you going to tell me about your gown?"

"What gown? I haven't made up my mind yet what I'm going to wear."

"Well," said Marguerite, "I have an idea. It is a bit wicked, but since he is the best, why not get one of Rojea's fabulous designs?"

Vivi was stunned. "How could you even think of such a thing, Marguerite, after knowing the fool he made of me?"

But Marguerite was determined to let her forget the past. "Come on, *cherie*. You were so young and foolish then. It is not your fault that he wasn't man enough to love you. But now you are in love, and you feel wonderful. Don't be afraid to show it."

"Marguerite," said Vivi, "your wisdom belies your years, and to prove to you that I'm not the same heartbroken child that left here a few months ago, I will do it."

Rojea was to design not only her gown, but almost her entire trousseau, and Vivi was radiant as she recounted the story to the DeVilles. The whole household was soon caught up in the excitement as packages arrived from the various shops.

Rojea had raved on about her beauty as usual, saying, "*Cherie*, you must be truly in love. I can see that certain glow, and I feel honored that you consider me worthy to do this. And so, for you I am going to create the most *magnifique* bridal gown ever seen by man."

Vivi was touched by his sincerity, and soon forgot what he was and the pain he had caused her. She felt free and happy that she would never have to go through such things again.

Meanwhile, Rojea envied her for being so much in love, but since there was nothing he could do to change himself, he vowed to do everything he could to ensure her happiness. He knew that was the least he could do after what he had done to her, so he volunteered to make Marguerite's gown as well. Marguerite hugged him as he took her measurements, and they all giggled and whispered like a bunch of school girls.

Before long there were fittings, and more fittings, such that Vivi became exhausted, but she rushed on and on as she made a mental picture of what their home was going to be like. In her mind she saw where every vase should be placed or every painting hung, and she could hardly wait to be Mrs. Ben DeVille.

It was agreed that Marguerite would take some of the things with her, while Vivi would ship the rest from New York.

After six weeks, Rojea delivered her gown, and she modeled it for the DeVilles that evening. "Oh, my *fille*," cried Comte Marselles DeVille, "you are the most beautiful bride since the Comtesse. That dress is so unique, it is you, Vivi, and I know you and my long-lost nephew will have a long and happy life together."

"Thank you, Uncle Marselles. Since my parents are gone, I have adopted you and Auntie Renee, so I think it fair to show you what I can, since you can't be there.

"*Merci, cherie.* We love you like our own daughter," said the countess, "and we want you to have this." It was the complete set of the DeVille pearls.

"But I couldn't accept this," said Vivi. "They are Marguerite's. She will marry someday, and I would feel guilty of cheating her of her birthright."

"No, *cherie.* You are marrying a DeVille, and this has been in their family for three generations. Please just consider it as something old."

"*Cherie,*" Marguerite said, "I will get the Lamont pearls. Don't worry. We are just so happy for you. Here, let me put them on."

With the finishing touch, Vivi was really a beautiful sight to behold, and since there was nothing they could say that would adequately describe their feelings, they all hugged her and cried.

A few days later, they all said another tearful goodbye, and Vivi returned to New York, where she made the final preparations for her wedding. She was now able to talk to Ben every day, and she looked forward to seeing him again. At first he was a little miffed at the fact she took so long, but he was so happy to hear her voice that he soon forgot all about that.

He said yes to everything she said, and when she asked his opinion on anything, he told her to do whatever she felt was right. "Vivi," he said, "all I want is to see you here with me. Nothing else really matters."

As her plans came together, she called Ben. "I will be home next weekend," she said.

"What?" he said. "How do you expect me to survive another week without you?"

"Don't worry, you will. Our future depends on it."

"Well, if you're sure I have no choice, but I suggest you tie up all loose ends while you're there, because I couldn't stand it if you were to go away again."

She promised she would. There was no easy way of telling him that one does not get rid of a sizeable fortune in a few days, or that it would be totally unnecessary.

Chapter Four

Van Anthony McNeil became heir to one of the largest furniture companies in New York at age twenty-one when both his parents were killed in a plane crash.

A student at Columbia University at the time, he had just decided he wanted to be a surgeon when he was forced to quit school and take control of his rather large inheritance. The New Rochelle home in which he had grown up was no more a haven for him; it was filled with memories more than he could bear. He could still hear his dear mother's voice or even her footsteps at times; for him living there was pure torture. He loved her so much and missed her terribly, but he also missed his father, though in a different way. They had not spent much time together, but he was sure his father loved him.

He felt as if his mother's eyes were always upon him and began to have awful dreams. That was when he decided to close the house and move to Manhattan. When he went to the lawyers concerning an apartment on Fifth Avenue, they thought him to be extravagant, but they understood his grief and made the purchase.

He chose the furnishings himself, and took nothing from his parents' house. He worked long hours and kept his mind busy with the business, refusing to face the fact that he was alone; they were never coming back. He even pretended they were at home. After it took him so long to make up his mind on a career, much to the disappointment of his father, he had finally chosen medicine, but now there was no need for that.

When work proved insufficient to obliterate the memories, he started drinking heavily. Then one day he visited one of the stores and met Vivianne Herron. She was almost petite, and had the most beautiful eyes he had ever seen. Suddenly he was talking to her, and before long, he knew she was the woman for him.

In college, the girls he met were all the same, and the few he ran around with after were just distraction from his pain. But Vivianne was different, and after a few dates, he proposed; and to his great shock and delight she accepted. Only then did he see a real reason to go on with his life, and he threw a huge engagement party.

Vivianne would soon finish her training as a surgical nurse, and they agreed that after graduation she would work until they started a family. She was twenty-one years old and he was twenty-four, but after the emptiness he had felt from the loss of his parents, he was ready to settle down.

A year after they met, they were married, and she moved into his Fifth Avenue apartment. Vivianne sensed his loneliness, and arranged her schedule so that she was always there for him when he came home. She didn't have to work anymore, but she felt bad letting her training go to waste, so she continued for three years. While attending parties and plays, they ate at all the important restaurants, and Van was so happy he gave up drinking, except socially.

One day while Vivianne was on her way to see a friend, she fainted and was rushed to the hospital where she worked. It didn't take long for the diagnosis to be made: she was pregnant. Van was overjoyed at the prospect of being a father. Taking her hand in his, he sat beside her and said, "Now that we've started, I think we will have six."

"Don't be so sure of that," she said. "Dr. Green suggests that I see an obstetrician right away, because he thinks there's a problem."

"What kind of a problem?"

"I'm not sure, but Dr. Threadwell is on his way, and he's one of the best in that field. Don't worry, Van, everything will be okay." In the days that followed, she wished she had tried to prepare her husband for the worst instead of reassuring him.

Dr. Threadwell was a tall, somber looking man with graying temples, and Vivianne wasn't sure whether it was due to her condition that he looked so alarmed or not, but when he spoke, she started breathing normally again.

"Mrs. McNeil," he said, "it will be necessary for us to run a few more tests, but at the moment, I suggest complete bed rest if you are to carry this child full term. Now, to ensure that, we are going to keep you here for a while, then we will be able to monitor your progress."

After her initial stay of one week, she was in and out of the hospital, and as the pregnancy progressed, the more obvious the risks became. But she was adamant. Knowing how much she wanted the baby, Dr. Threadwell sought advice from his colleagues, but they all agreed that it was dangerous for her to continue. She told Van she was going to have her baby regardless of the consequences, and he knew she was trying to be brave, but could he stand the loss of another loved one?

He was petrified. Desperately, he tried to reason with her, but she told him she could not agree for them to destroy her baby. "Since the child is healthy, I want to give it a chance to live, and if I don't, you will have a part of me. The child will be the product of our love."

"Our love? Is it because you love me that you are so anxious to sacrifice yourself for an unborn child? Have you given any thought to what would happen to me if I should lose you?"

"Van," she said, "we are talking about two lives: mine and my baby's. Who is going to judge which is more important?"

There was a hint of resignation in her voice, and it was quite clear to him that there was nothing he could say to change her mind. His only other hope was to try and get Dr. Threadwell as an ally, but he told him that there was no certainty that he could save her by taking the child. "Mr. McNeil," he said, "your wife is seriously ill. There are complications, and she also has a heart murmur. I think she has known this for some time but refused to cause you any more grief. We will be doing our best, and as soon as she completes her seventh month, we are going to take the child. At that point it will be fully developed and able to survive, but right now she is more of a problem."

"Dr. Threadwell," said Van, "if there is need for a choice between her and the child, save my wife."

He went back to her room and found her in terrible pain. "How are you, honey?"

"Fine, but the baby is kicking, I think. . . ."

She screamed, a nurse came running and within minutes there were doctors. "I think she's ready," said Dr. Threadwell. "Let's get her to OR."

Van went with her as far as he was allowed to go, kissed her and said, "I know you can do it, honey, and I'll be right here if you need me."

"Mr. McNeil," said the nurse, "I'm sorry, but you have to go now. We can't waste any time."

An hour later, Dr. Threadwell reappeared. "You have a daughter," he said, "but both she and your wife are very weak. As soon as she goes back to recovery, you can see her, but just for a minute. I must go now."

Van was somewhat relieved, but there was that look of doubt on the doctor's face that made him uneasy. When he was able to see her, she was sleeping, but she looked fine to him and he began to hope that they would both survive, although the baby was tiny and in an incubator. As long as there was a chance, he would cling to it, because life couldn't be so cruel to him. After all, he hadn't done anything to deserve that. "I'll be back," he said, although he knew she was too drugged and sleepy to hear or respond.

It was several hours before she awoke, and she was very weak, but she asked to see her baby.

"She's okay," said the nurse, "but since she was premature, she's in an incubator. By the time you're able to get out of bed, she should be ready to go home."

"No, I have to hold her, and I need to see my husband. There's not much time. Please let me see her."

She soon fell asleep again, but the nurse was worried about her and called the doctor on duty to have a look at her. "We have to monitor her closely, nurse, but there's nothing to do now but wait and give her whatever she asks for to keep her calm."

"But she wants to see her baby."

"Tomorrow I'll arrange for her to be brought in for a few minutes. By the way, how is the baby?"

"Pretty good, doctor. She's just tiny."

"Good. If her condition changes, I'll be here."

Vivianne was still very weak, but when she saw her baby, her face almost lit up. "My little girl," she whispered as she checked her fingers and toes to be sure she was perfect. "Oh Van!" she said, "I'm glad she's alive. I want you to call her Vivi."

Van was struggling with his feelings; he wasn't sure he wanted to see the baby – not if it meant loosing his wife. But from her detached manner of speaking, it was evident that she was resigned to the inevitable, and expected him to be the same.

"Oh honey," she was saying, "she will always be a part of us, and you shouldn't blame her. I wasn't as strong as we thought, but I'm leaving someone for you to care for."

The doctors did all they could, but her heart stopped, and three days after Vivianne Heron McNeil gave birth, she died.

***

Except for his baby daughter, Van McNeil was alone for the second time in his life, and he wanted no part of her. Since there was no relative in this country, he decided to hire a nanny who would provide the mother figure that the child would need.

One of the nurses told him of a reputable agency, and he started setting up interviews, but no one suited him until finally, there was Miss Francis, whose references seemed okay. And after he explained the requirements of the position, she was delighted to take on the responsibility. She was English, and he saw that she was compassionate; something in her reminded him of his dear mother.

"Miss Francis," he said, "I want you to understand that you will be in complete control of everything that concerns the baby. I need your word that you will treat her as if she were your own."

"Of course, Mr. McNeil! I have been a nanny all my adult life, and I have worked in some of the finest homes in this country, as you have verified. It will be both my duty and a pleasure to care for her."

"Thank you very much. In two days she will be released from the hospital. That should give you enough time to get settled in."

Nanny Francis, as she was affectionately called by the children she had cared for previously, was a kind woman, and her heart went out to the man she was going to work for. She could tell he was a young man, but the pain in his eyes belied his years. How could he have known such grief, being wealthy? Though he had just lost his wife, there had to be more to his obvious suffering.

In order to protect him, she asked the maid to put away all Mrs. McNeil's personal belongings so they wouldn't be a constant reminder to her husband, and although she didn't see him often, when she did, she kept out of his way.

He did not go with her for the baby, as she had been led to believe. Instead, he sent his chauffeur to take her. The nurses seemed sad and a bit reluctant to give the baby up, but as Nanny took her and cuddled the little bundle, they realized she was in good hands.

Van refused to see his daughter, and felt terribly ashamed of his action, but he resented her for living while causing the death of her mother. He didn't know her, but he had known and loved his wife, who had kept him from being so alone. What would he do without Vivianne, and what could the baby do for him? He was tormented with questions to which there were no answers, and he turned again to the only thing that helped him to forget: alcohol.

His confusion heightened as he tried to understand what Vivianne told him about "life," because he still wasn't sure what she meant. And soon his inability to fathom the reason for the tragic existence he led made him bitter. He was angry, and not having anyone else at whom he could direct his wrath, he directed it at his baby daughter.

He seldom went home, and when he did, he was too drunk to see anyone, and he didn't want to. Somewhere in his twisted mind, he truly resented the baby for taking away his beloved Vivianne. Now why should he worry about her, he thought to himself.

His bitterness continued for several months, and by this time Nanny Francis was more than a little worried. about him. She prayed he would come home one night at a decent hour so she could confront him. She agreed that he missed his wife, but avoiding the baby wasn't the answer, and she was going to give him a piece of her mind the very next time he set foot in the house.

On December twenty-first she called his office and left a message that she needed to see him. When he didn't call to find out what she wanted, she waited up for him. At about eleven o'clock, he walked in, all haggard and disheveled. Her heart sank. He looked old beyond his years, and she dreaded what she was about to do. How could she attack that wretched looking creature who looked at her with almost unseeing eyes? But if she didn't, things might get worse.

She got up and went to him. "Mr. McNeil, may I speak to you frankly?"

"Sure, Nanny, what is it?"

"Well, sir, it is about your daughter."

"My daughter? Is anything wrong with her?"

"I guess you could say so, sir. She needs a father."

"I am her father, but you can't expect me to sit around here all day. That's why I hired you."

"Granted, sir, but did you know she's able to say 'Da-di' and that she crawls around the house as if looking for someone besides me?"

"How could she? She doesn't even know me."

"That's just it, sir. She says it because I taught her to, not because she knows you."

Meanwhile, as she rambled on, all he could hear was his own voice saying, "She doesn't even know me."

Nanny said, "I'm sorry, sir, but I'm afraid I must retire. Is there anything I can do for you, even though it's way past my bedtime?"

He didn't hear her as he headed for the nursery, where he knelt at his daughter's crib and cried as if his very heart was breaking. Through the tears, he told the sleeping child all his feelings against her and pleaded for her forgiveness. "My poor innocent baby. When did you grow up so, and where was I? Can you ever forgive me for not being here? I was hurting so bad I couldn't love you like I should, but I promise I will make it up to you." He touched her face and all he saw was a smaller version of Vivianne. "You even look like your mother. From this day on I will always be here when you need me."

Nanny, not wanting to intrude, pretended to be asleep in the adjoining room, but she cried as much as he and was glad to know he reconciled with his daughter.

Van slept late the next day, and when he got up, he called his secretary to say he wouldn't be in. For the first time in months, he felt at home as he showered and shaved, then dressed for breakfast. Nanny was delighted to see him looking somewhat normal, and hoped her lecture had made a permanent difference in his life. Haltingly he asked, "Is the baby still asleep, Nanny?"

"Oh, no, Mr. McNeil. We will be going for a stroll in a little while, and she is all ready and waiting."

"Do you mind if I take her today?"

"I really don't mind, sir, but I doubt that you could manage on your own."

"Well, then, may I just tag along?"

"Mr. McNeil, we will be very happy to have you along," she beamed as she hurried from the room.

He got up and walked to the nursery, and there in her play pen stood the most beautiful little baby girl he had ever seen. He was afraid to approach her, thinking he might frighten her, but he couldn't resist, and when she saw him, she just smiled and held up her hands to be picked up. "Oh, my angel," he crooned as he held her to his breast. "You are so beautiful, and I almost missed you growing up." Soon Nanny appeared, and they headed for the street, where several heads were turned as he proudly walked beside his daughter.

For Christmas he bought a tree, and Nanny was happy to help him decorate it. "I want this Christmas to be special for her, Nanny. I want to thank you for bringing me to my senses before it was too late. Since I have no close relatives, I hope you will always be a part of this household, not just for Vivi, but for me as well."

"Well, sir, I never planned on going anywhere until she is married, which I think will be a few years yet."

They laughed, and when the tree was finished, they were astonished at how good a job they had done.

On Christmas Eve, Van lit the tree with his daughter in his arms and watched her as she gazed in amazement. At nine months old, he didn't expect her to know the full meaning of it, but it was something he had to do, to try and compensate for all the times he had neglected her.

Nanny was shocked at the mountain of packages under the tree, but she understood what was happening to him, and when the time came to open them, she helped gladly. But the biggest shock of all was when she got to an envelope bearing her name. She looked at her employer suspiciously as she opened it; it contained a check for five thousand dollars. "Mr. McNeil, I can't accept this. I don't understand why you feel you should do this, but I like to earn whatever I receive."

"Nanny, there is no need for you to get upset. To me, you have earned more than that. You stood by me when I was so confused, and took care of my daughter without any help from me. And then it was your words that brought me to my senses in the end. For services like that, one cannot really pay adequately in cash, but all I'm trying to do is thank you." He hugged his daughter who was sitting on his lap biting on one of her new toys, and as Nanny watched them together, she thought if she did bring such happiness to him, maybe she did deserve a reward.

She got up and brushed the tinsel from her dress. "Thank you very much, Mr. McNeil. I love the sweater too, and I do wish you a merry Christmas, sir." A carol was playing and she hummed along happily as she proceeded to rid the room of all the wrappings from the gifts, which all but two belonged to Vivi.

Van spent his first Christmas with his daughter then, and that was the beginning of a new life for him. He no longer wandered around town with his drinking partners; he had a purpose, someone to live for, and he was determined to be the best father there ever was to her.

For her third birthday, he opened up the house in New Rochelle and gave her a party. He wanted her to have room to play, now that she was able to run and be outdoors with other children. Then came her fourth birthday, and he bought her a pony, which she called "Horsey" the moment she set eyes on it. Nanny suggested they find a real name for the poor animal, but Van was adamant. "It's hers. If she wants to call it Horsey, so be it."

They spent summers in New Rochelle and winters in Manhattan. They were always together, and Van's social life became almost nonexistent. A few years back he had promoted his assistant to manager, in order to have some time for himself, and the law firm of Agar & Phipps still handled all the legal matters, just as his father had left them. He seemed to have lost interest in everything and everyone except his daughter, till one day he said to Nanny, "Vivi needs a mother. I think I'm going to get married."

Nanny was annoyed, and she didn't hesitate to show it. "Sir, if you will forgive me, I take good care of Vivi. If you want to get married, do it for yourself, but not for her."

"Okay, Nanny, don't get so upset. It's bad for the heart. I will take your advice." He had gotten to know her over the years and liked to tease her sometimes, but he was lucky to have her, and he wanted her to be happy. After all, she was almost like a mother to Vivi, and he owed her more than any other person in the world.

From that day, he never mentioned marriage to her again, and although he had several affairs, he never brought any of the women home. He became one the most eligible bachelors again, and there were many attempts to take him to the altar, but he was afraid to take the plunge. He enjoyed himself, but there was still an empty space in his heart, and he knew he had to settle down. But could he find anyone who would be willing to take second place in his life?

The years passed swiftly, and Van enjoyed his little girl to the fullest. She was all he really cared about, and he spent every moment he could with her. He took her to ball games, Coney Island, the zoo and everywhere of importance to a child. They rode the subways and sometimes stood in the front car and watch as the train wormed its way through the maze of tracks. She would scream with delight when they emerged from the semi-darkness of the underground to a burst of sunlight on the elevated lines.

Van showered her with gifts. She had dolls, a doll house, and toys of all shapes and sizes, but she seemed more interested in reading, and he was very proud of her. It appeared as if she had a new question for him every day, and he was truly amazed at her powers of imagination as well as understanding.

She played with the neighbors' children, but her best friend was Mary Flint, one of her English teacher's daughters. Mary would come and spend weekends with her, but she was never allowed to go out without being under her father's or Nanny Francis's watchful eyes.

Chapter Five

At age eleven, Vivi was introduced to French by one of her teachers, and was fascinated with the language. She began reading books about France, and asked her father to take her there sometime. "You promise, Daddy?"

"Of course, angel. I might even send you to school there if you behave, but that's when you're older."

"Gee, Daddy! You're the best."

"You really mean that, angel?"

She hugged him, and once more he knew the joy of having such a loving child. If only her mother had lived to share her love. Although he tried to think of his wife as little as possible, she was never really too far from him.

He had recently met Tessie Lagossa, a dancer, and asked her to marry him. She told him she needed time to think about it, but he suspected she only needed enough time to find out how wealthy he was. He liked her because she made him laugh and she was beautiful. The fact that she wasn't a society girl didn't bother him much. He needed love, and if she could give it to him, he would try to go on with his life.

Later, when he told Vivi, she agreed to meet her, but he could see she wasn't exactly thrilled at the prospect. After the initial meeting, Van might have changed his mind, but Tessie proudly announced to him that she was pregnant. So, almost twelve years after Vivianne's death, he married

Tessie Lagossa. He wanted to do the right thing, and it never entered his mind she might be lying or that she had no intention of spoiling her figure. Vivi was as close as she was going to come to being a mother, and she even had a nanny.

Unfortunately for Tessie, things didn't always go as planned, for the child resented her in every possible way, and even Nanny was just civil to her. But all evidence pointed to the fact that they didn't want her there. She was so bored and lonely during the days, she soon started shopping every day. After a couple of months, one night in bed, Van seized the opportunity to ask her, "Honey, do you know anything about a bill from Sak's for two thousand dollars?"

"Yes, darling, I saw this adorable dress and I just had to get it."

"Okay, sweetheart, do me a favor. Tell me how many other stores you've been to." And as she named them, his temper rose, and he took her by the shoulders and began to shake her. "What on earth are you trying to do to me? Do you want to see me go broke? If you spend so much in two months, how many fortunes do you think I have?"

Her eyes were wild and she glared at him. "What do you expect me to do? You leave me here in what is supposed to be my home, and nobody even talks to me. The woman treats me like dirt, and that brat of yours acts as if I'm dung."

Before Van knew what was happening, he had slapped her face. "Never refer to Vivi as a brat again, never. You hear me?" shaking her as he screamed. "You no-good, lying slut, you lied to me from the very beginning, which means this whole marriage is a lie."

She began to shake as she realized what he was saying; he had finally found out she wasn't pregnant, and if he should take her to court, she could lose everything. "Oh, Van, I didn't mean to lie to you. I really thought I was pregnant."

"Yes, and when did you find out that you weren't?"

"Just a few days ago."

"Like hell you did. If that were so, why didn't you tell me?"

"I . . . I was afraid."

"Afraid of what?"

"Just what is happening now, and so you can see I was right."

"And who are you going to blame for all this? Oh, God, I never believed you were such a scheming tramp."

That was the beginning of a series of quarrels which always ended with insults being thrown at each other. They made up, it seemed, just long enough to start another fight, and Tessie just couldn't live like that. She started to visit her old haunts, and would sometimes spend the day with whomever was willing or able. In her misery, she turned to her girlfriend Linda for advice. "Oh Linda, I don't know what to do. Since he found out that I lied to him about being pregnant, he hates me. Then the child doesn't even know I'm alive."

"But Tessie," said Linda, "was it necessary to lie? You knew he loved you, or at least he had already asked you to marry him."

"Yes, but when I found out who he was and thought he might have been drunk when he asked me, I made up the story so he wouldn't change his mind."

"Tessie," said Linda, "I wasn't going to say this, but I can't help reminding you that your greed always gets you in trouble. Everybody who knows Van McNeil knows that his daughter is his pride and joy. What you ought to be doing is trying to win her affection. Then he will see you in a different light. Use your head, Tessie. The way to Van McNeil's heart and his fortune is through his daughter."

"Thank you, Linda. You are a good friend, and I'm going to get to that brat if it kills me. As soon as I get home, I'm going to ask her to call me Mother."

Linda stared at her in disbelief as she tried to compose herself from the laughter that gushed out of her.

"You know, it's a brilliant idea," said Tessie. "I think I will suggest it at dinner." She couldn't wait to get home, and once she did, she couldn't wait till dinner. She found Vivi and Nanny practicing some French words, and said, "Vivi, I would like to speak with you." She totally ignored Nanny Francis, and Vivi made a mental note of that as Nanny excused herself.

"Well, Vivi, I hardly know how to say this, but I would truly like for us to be friends, since we have to live together and I'm married to your father. Do you think you could begin calling me Mother?"

"Mother!" Vivi stood up. "My mother is dead, and I will never call you that. Since you came here, I don't see Daddy anymore. I hate you. I hate you!" she screamed as she bounded up the stairs and into her room, slamming the door.

Not knowing that her father was home and heard the whole conversation, when he knocked on her door, she refused to open it until he called, "Vivi, it's me."

She ran to him and he hugged her, but in his heart he knew he had to do something permanent about the utter resentment between his wife and daughter. "Honey, it's okay, I'm here now. Do you remember some time ago we discussed your going away to school?" He hesitated. "Do you still want to go?"

"Daddy, are you sending me away because of her?"

"No, darling. Be reasonable. When we talked about that, she wasn't even here yet."

Vivi was silent as she thought of the possibilities of going away, and she acquiesced and began wiping the tears from her eyes.

Her father was relieved. "Okay, that's my girl. Now go and make yourself beautiful for me. It's almost time for dinner."

There was the usual hush at dinner until Tessie said, "Van, why don't we all take a vacation? You've always said Vivi wants to go to Paris, and I wouldn't mind it myself, so why don't we all go?"

Even at age thirteen, Vivi knew what was happening, but then it might be to her advantage, so why not? "Yes, Daddy!" she chimed in, "but only if Nanny goes too."

"Of course, honey. Where you go, Nanny goes, and if you like it, you can stay there and finish school."

"Oh, Daddy, you're the best! I'm quite sure I am going to like it there."

Van tried to sound elated. "Now that it's settled, I will make the necessary arrangements and we can all have some fun."

Tessie sighed. "Thank God we all agree on something in this family. I do consider this a major achievement."

Ignoring her sarcasm, Van said, "There is just one problem with this arrangement, honey. I detest flying and I don't think I can go by ship, so I might not be able to accompany you after all."

Vivi started to laugh and said, "You, Daddy, afraid?" Then she remembered that he had told her his parents died in a plane crash. "Oh, Daddy, I'm sorry. I didn't mean to laugh. I forgot about Grandma and Grandpa."

"I know, honey, but tell you what. I'm going with you. Don't forget, Vivi, I will do anything for you, anything that will make you happy."

***

Three weeks after the inception of the plan, they boarded the plane at Kennedy Airport, each with their own objective and hope that they would be justified. To Vivi it was an adventure far beyond her childish expectations.

Her father took her first to see the Eiffel Tower, and to all the scenery that was Paris. After two weeks at the Hotel Bristol, he began to look for a permanent residence for her. He found a sort of country-style chateau in the heart of Paris, close to the Seine. It wasn't in the best part of the city, but it was convenient for the Metro, cafés, libraries, theatre and almost anything she would need.

The adjustment was difficult at first, but soon she understood the differences. There were words like "madeleine" that appeared in so many different contexts —

she was so surprised that she even wrote to tell one of her little schoolmates in America that in France her name meant 'bun,' 'tea cake,' 'early pear' and a host of other things she didn't even understand.

Her father found her a private school, and with the help of Nanny Francis, she soon settled in. Seeing she had a propensity for languages, she studied one after the other, and within four years was fluent in German, Russian and Japanese, in addition to French and English.

At seventeen, she began spending more time with her classmate Marguerite and would go to the Chateau Lamont, where Marguerite lived with her parents. Before long, they were almost inseparable. They went on excursions together and even went to the zoo to make up for the time they spent studying.

However, it was time for her to consider a career, so she enrolled in college, where she could decide on what she was going to do. There were times when she felt she would rather be free, but she went, after Marguerite convinced her it was the thing to do. To Vivi, the culture was the most fascinating thing about Paris, and France on a whole.

One day Marguerite said, "Why do we bore ourselves with school when there's so much to see? We are heiresses. What we should be doing is spending our money. Or maybe marry some rich man and spend his money." They both laughed.

"Well," said Vivi, "my only ambition is to be a linguist."

"Yeah?"

"Yes, be an interpreter for some foreign dignitary."

"Now, you see, we can have fun and really see this country."

From then on they went to galleries, sightseeing at the Louvre, where they discovered Roman, Egyptian, Oriental and other antiquities. Vivi was also convinced that Parisian churches were the most beautiful in the world.

When she was a child, Nanny Francis had taught her to pray, and later explained to her the importance of being chaste. She sang Psalms to her and the times they spent in church were filled with such reverence and wonder. She could still hear Nanny singing from the psalter, proudly imitating her father, who she said was the greatest baritone and choirmaster in all of the Church of England.

"Your daddy," Nanny would end her talks sadly, "was a wonderful man, but he gave in to drinking, or he might be alive today." That was when Vivi would vow all over again not to touch alcohol.

"Dear Nanny," she sighed. "What would I have done without you?"

She felt drawn to those Gothic buildings with their domes and stained glass, and she visited them on a regular basis. She and Marguerite played tennis, and shopped, and spent time at the Chateau DeVille in Marseilles whenever they felt like a vacation.

Then one day after their return, Madame Lamont-DeVille invited her to join them for dinner and the opera. Marguerite was thrilled, mostly because it gave her reason to shop. She took Vivi to Rojea Molen and they bought so much, it had to be sent to them. Vivi thought he was the most handsome man she had ever met, and immediately fell for him. She had no knowledge that he had no real interest in her, but would use her to confuse his critics.

Rojea Molen, the famous designer, needed the public to see him with rich young ladies. And Vivi, with Marguerite as chaperone, was often such a young lady. He enjoyed making grand entrances with the two beauties, one on each arm, knowing he was the envy of all his competitors.

***

Arriving in Paris again, Vivi almost felt like a child again. She remembered how she and Nanny Francis spent their first year getting acquainted with the customs, the cuisine and the overall lifestyle. But she was reminded also of the trips she had taken to spend the holidays with her father – especially the Christmas that she came home to find her father divorced, and Tessie gone.

Now she was getting married. Closing her eyes, she could see her father standing there when the minister said, "Who gives this woman to be married to this man?" and hear him proudly saying, "I do."

It was strange, but of all the girls she had met, her only true friend was Marguerite. Vivi smiled as she thought how Marguerite acted as wisdom itself, although she was only two years her senior. She pretended to have the answer to every problem, but they certainly had fun together. Now, by a twist of fate, they were going to be related by marriage. Vivi was always aware that there was a force that governs man's destiny, and now she was positive that without its intervention, her life would not have been so good.

She had written to Nanny of her intention to marry, and Nanny sent her blessings, but said she was unable to attend since her sister had taken a turn for the worse. With no one else, Vivi's whole life was centered around the

DeVille family, and she planned to live up to their expectations and keep their friendship.

She almost expected to see her father standing there when she opened her eyes, but he was gone, and she had to accept that. When she did fall asleep, she dreamed she saw him. And as she called him, "Daddy . . . Daddy," and finally caught up with him, when he turned to face her, it wasn't her father. Instead she was looking at the smiling face of Ben DeVille.

The dream brought her sadness too, memories of the day they received that terrible phone call. "Miss Vivi," cook had said, "I'm sorry, but they called to say your father had a heart attack earlier today, and before the doctors could try to help him, he was gone." It was a nightmare, she remembered. However, she didn't cry because she was sure it was a mistake. Somehow she had thought when they checked, they would discover it wasn't him. But it was him. Nanny had made the travel arrangements, and Vivi was faced with the reality of it all. She was only eighteen years old and an orphan.

Then six months later, Nanny Francis had to return to England to care for her ailing sister. She was completely alone, except for the friendship of Marguerite DeVille and her parents, the Comte and Comtesse.

Chapter Six

Vivi awoke earlier than usual and was blissfully aware that it was her wedding day. She still missed having a relative to share in her happiness, but Marguerite would have to suffice, since she was all she had. She had arrived two days earlier and spent most of her time sleeping after the long trip. Vivi didn't want to think about anything, and she knew just what she needed.

She donned her bathing suit and started toward the beach, which to her surprise was already crowded. She dived in and felt a calmness sweep over her as the soothing water rushed against her body. When she surfaced, she had a feeling she was being watched, but she ignored it and took a second dive and came face to face with Ben under the water. He held her and they came up together. "Ben! What are you doing here?"

"Well, I wanted to see you, and I had a feeling you would be here, so here I am." He kissed her.

"Ben DeVille, I can't believe you are really spying on me."

"I have no need to, love. The people of this town look after their own, and you are one of us now."

"Don't you be so sure of that," she teased. "I can still change my mind."

"Would you?"

"Not a chance." She kissed him. "I am almost twenty-one years old. It's about time I find out what I have been missing."

She jumped back in the water and he followed and they were like children as they anticipated the future together. Suddenly she remembered, "Ben! Do you know it's bad luck to see your bride before the wedding?"

"What?"

"Annie said so."

"Well, I don't know about that, but one thing I know – I have waited all my life for this day, and I'm glad you are willing to share it with me."

"It is not because I'm willing that I have consented to marry you, Ben. It's because I love you, and I hope you never forget it."

"I love you too, Vivi, even when you are serious."

"Look, Ben, I don't know whether it means anything or not, but I would rather not find out. Get out of here and let me go get dressed. I have an appointment with the hairdresser."

"Kiss me before I go. I will always remember the night you said yes, you would marry me, and now the day is finally here. I hope you will never have cause to regret. I will always love you, and treasure the times we spend together."

Ben left and Vivi found herself mulling over her activities the day before. She had seen to the menu and, with Annie's help, all the decorations were in place. They had worked well into the night, and Vivi had given it all she had. There were vases of the most beautiful flowers everywhere, but she had a special fondness for anthuriums, and she decked the master bedroom with them. With the aid of Annie's crew, they hung new lace curtains with matching bedspreads and shams, all the little touches that gave the place an aura of femininity.

The great hall in which the reception would be held was done in white, and she supervised it all in order to assure it was just right. There were pots and bowls of flowers everywhere, the tables were covered with fine lace, and each place setting had a long-stemmed red rose, of silk so it would not fade in the heat.

Ben's friends had given him a bachelor party, and it was Ross's duty to keep him away from that section of the house. With Annie and Ross, the conspiracy went well and Vivi was relieved. Her only problem was the heat – she was afraid the flowers would fade, but she had no choice. In her mind she had succeeded in planning a beautiful wedding and she hoped Ben would be delighted at the changes she had made. With all the questions answered, she was free to marry him and hoped she wouldn't disappoint him with her inexperience, but be the kind of wife he deserved.

Meanwhile, Ben went home and Annie ushered him into one of the guest rooms. He wondered what was going on. "Annie, why am I in this room? And why are the doors locked?"

"Well, Mr. Ben, you know we have to prepare for your weddin', and I for one, don't want anybody in there messin' up things. Anyway, if you can keep a secret, I am goin' to show you the handiwork of that little gem you are about to marry." Annie opened the door and Ben looked in utter amazement at what used to be his bedroom. He walked from room to room with his mouth opened, but no sound came, and then she let him out to the hall where he finally said, "This is incredible. When was this done?"

"Well, Mr. Ben, while you were out galvantin' last night, we were busy workin'."

"You mean Vivi did all this?"

"It's about time you know that we women stick together and she is better than all the others you ever had put together."

Ben was in awe of Vivi's creativity, but also he knew she must have spent a fortune. Who was Vivi McNeil anyway? Was there more to her than she let be known?

Annie saw that he was puzzled, but she immediately took his silence for disapproval and decided to scold him. "You don't have to look like that, Mr. Ben. It is goin' to be her home too. She has a right to do things how she likes it."

Ben surprised her as he picked her up and said, "Annie, you want to know what I think? I think she's the most wonderful woman in the world, and you are next."

He gave her a peck on the cheek and started for the door, but Annie was wise to him. "And where do you think you are goin'? It is bad luck for the groom to see the bride before the weddin'."

He fixed himself a drink and went to the room he was staying in, but his thoughts went back to the conversation he had with Vivi the day before. She said she didn't like to keep secrets and had asked him about his relationship to Ross. "Ben, there is just one more thing I have to know." She took a deep breath and said, "What is your relationship to Ross?"

He couldn't imagine then what she was thinking, but he had held her and told her, "He's my half-brother."

Somehow he always knew she was curious, and her reaction to his reply had confirmed his suspicion. "Your brother? Ross is your brother? Oh my God! Why on earth didn't you tell me? Why all the secrecy?"

"Well, he was my mother's illegitimate son, and on account of him, Mother was ostracized from society. Ever since we found out, we agreed to keep it quiet so that her memory wouldn't be dragged in the mud here also."

"I'm sorry, Ben. I didn't mean to pry. It's just that I was afraid you might be otherwise involved, since I couldn't see the connection."

Even the thought of her insinuation made him sick, but when she told him her story of Rojea and her involvement with him, he understood her fears. But the part of the conversation that stood out in his mind was when she said, "Why on earth didn't you tell me?" That single question reverberated in his mind, and he knew unless he saw her and got it over with, those words would come back to haunt him.

His drink untouched, he hurried out the back way. He must tell her before he married her, but he was afraid she might change her mind. He told himself he was doing the right thing, but when he arrived, Marguerite was there.

"Ben! What are you doing here?"

"I have to see Vivi."

"Oh, no you don't!"

"Look, Marguerite, there is something I have to tell her."

"Yes, my dear cousin, but it will have to wait. I have my orders not to let you in."

"Okay, may I speak to her with the door closed?"

"All right, go ahead." But by the time he reached the door, he knew it was too late then, and when she answered, he said, "I came to tell you that I have seen the house and I love you."

He was troubled when he left her and he remembered the day when she had sounded so mysterious. "Ben, there are things about me you don't know." She got up and turned her back to him as she said, "I'm a virgin." She was afraid to admit it, he guessed, but he had suspected it all along and loved her more for it.

He had dried her tears and saw that she was embarrassed to discuss such things with him, but he meant it when he told her, "Love! That's the most wonderful thing to happen to a woman on her wedding day."

She was truly unspoiled and loving and understanding; she even insisted that Ross give her away instead of Deacon Johnson. Eventually the two men switched places in order that she might get her wish. Everything was going fine. Why should he do anything that might intrude on her happiness?

Ben DeVille was a very cautious man by nature, but for the first time in his life, he was allowing himself to relax. He was deeply in love with Vivi and had all the evidences that proved she loved him too. She had beauty, brains, and the kind of upbringing that would make any man proud to have her as his wife and the mother of his children. He planned to help her in becoming the most famous hostess on the island. With her grace and charm, and his money and social standing, he could almost assure her happiness. He never discussed it with her; he just assumed that was the role he wanted her to play and she would readily accept.

He planned to keep her away from the people who might say the wrong things to her, because he wasn't going to see her hurt. His duty was to protect her, and he would do it with his last breath, until he had an opportunity to sit her down and tell her how it all happened. She loved him, and she would surely understand his reluctance to mention it before.

***

Annie sighed. She loved Ben like her own son, and after all his misfortunes with women as well as his parents, she was glad he had found happiness. After his father's death, he sold the house in Kingston and concentrated on the West Palm estate.

She had taken care of him since he was born, and although he didn't exactly resemble his mother, there were things about him that always reminded her of her — sweet Jeanette, so delicate yet strong, with the most beautiful green eyes she ever saw. She was a good woman, and Annie often wondered how she could marry a lout like Jacques DeVille. His cruelty to his wife always caused her to think of him as Jack The Ripper instead of his real name.

Eventually she sought refuge in the arms of the only available man at the time, who turned out to be the no-good Red Treveck. Red was a known ladies man who never married, but poor Jeanette never saw him that way. To her he was there when she needed him, and that was all that mattered.

Jack spent weeks away from home gambling and visiting brothels, and whenever he returned home, he abused her both verbally and physically until, out of loneliness, she turned to Red and soon became pregnant.

She was horrified at first, but after much thought, she felt she was getting even with her husband and just waited for him to ask her about her condition. When he did ask her, she told him if he were a real husband to her, he would have no need to ask. "After all I'm your wife!" she yelled.

He had struck her then and she fell against a chest where Annie found her a few moments later and took her to her room. To her surprise, her mistress was in an advanced state of pregnancy which could no longer be hidden, and if Annie didn't get her breathing normally again, the child might be in danger. She grabbed a pitcher of water from the washstand and threw in it in her face full force, and immediately she stirred and reached for the side of her head. There was a slight contusion, and Annie sent one of the other servants to fetch Dr. Grey, who treated the wound and gave her a mild sedative.

Two months later, she gave birth to a nine-pound, four-ounce baby boy, and when her husband saw the child, he ordered her out of the house. But Red was ahead of Jack and soon presented Jeanette with the deed to the West Palm estate in Savanna-la-Mar. While Jack was out on one of his famous trips, Jeanette took the children and everything she wanted from the house and moved to her own place, with Red posing as her guest.

It took a while for Jack to find her, and when he did, he demanded that she give him his son. She was devastated, but knowing the law would be on his side, she agreed. How quickly things had changed from the day Ben was born when there was such a celebration.

It pained Annie so as she watched her mistress and friend suffering and tried to give her solace, but to no avail. There was always that distant look in her eyes which had suddenly gone pale.

Jacques stayed away longer each time he left, and the last time they saw him was when he took Ben. Before he left, he told her he never wanted to see her or her bastard again, and ironically he didn't. Five years after Jack took Ben, Jeanette died of tuberculosis, according to the doctor, but Annie knew how much she missed her son and always suspected that she was so brokenhearted she lost the will to live.

Ben was allowed to attend his mother's funeral and somehow he never returned home to his father. Annie had loved Jeanette and she took care of her sons for her after her death. Ben was then seventeen and Ross was almost six. She gave them all the love she could and she was proud to see the way they turned out.

There was someone at the door, and Annie remembered what she was about to do. She had the hired cooks to supervise and a bride to attend. How could she be daydreamin' at a time like this, she wondered to herself, and ran hastily toward the door.

She was tickled as she remembered the column in the *Gleaner:* "Sugarcane magnate Ben DeVille of Westmoreland to marry princess of undisclosed province, according to the grapevine." She was as proud of them as if they were her own children. And she thanked the grapevine, whoever they were. But she'd better be on her way. As her father used to say, "Annie, time and tide wait for no man."

***

Vivi was dressed only in her undergarments when she heard a knock on her door, and believing it to be Marguerite, she said, "Come in."

Ben hurried in and closed the door behind him.

"Ben! What are you doing here?"

"I have a surprise for you. Pack whatever you think you are going to need. I'm taking you to one of the most fabulous places for our honeymoon."

"Oh, Ben, I love you, but get out. Annie will be here soon, and you shouldn't be."

"Is that all you're going to wear?" he teased.

"Yes, Ben. If you don't leave, I just might."

Marguerite entered the room, and he stole a kiss from his bride-to-be and ran down the stairs. In a few seconds they heard the roar of his car engine and all they could do was look at each other.

"Marguerite, I want to thank you for introducing me to Ben, for even though he acts crazy at times, I think he's the most wonderful man in the world. I do owe everything to you and wish you and Claude will be as happy as we are, although I notice you haven't said much about him since you arrived. Is there a problem?"

"Oh, *cherie*, this is no time for you to be thinking about me. This is your wedding day, a day to be cherished by the both of you. You know his father was the proverbial black sheep of the family, but I love my cousin and I love you too. I'm just glad that the two of you found happiness."

"Thank you, Marguerite. This is truly the most important day of my life and I hope to enjoy it to its fullest." She sat down and turned her thoughts to Ben. She believed he really loved her and she was certain she loved him, so why was she in doubt? The fact that she was inexperienced still haunted her. What if she didn't measure up to his expectations? If only her mother had lived, she would have taught her things she should know instead of her depending on books for her information. Well, there was no turning back now. Her fear of men would leave her sometime, and after all, Ben was different.

"Come on, Vivi," Marguerite called from the other room. "I bet you haven't even done your makeup. What's the matter? Annie will soon be here to help you get dressed."

"I'm afraid, Marguerite."

"Afraid of what, *cherie*?"

"Well, I know how much Ben is looking forward to this day. What if I disappoint him?"

"You will be just fine. If you didn't feel like this, it would be somewhat abnormal. Brides are supposed to feel like this, *cherie*. You love Ben, don't you?"

"Yes, I do."

"And you believe he loves you?"

"Yes. To be honest with you, at times when he looks at me, it is with such admiration that it worries me that I might not measure up."

"Why worry about simple things, *cherie,* when you have the most important ingredient, your love for each other."

"Oh, Marguerite." Vivi hugged her friend. "I don't know what I would do without you. You are the soul of experience. Where did you learn all that?"

"You really don't want to know that, *cherie*."

Vivi started to laugh. "You sounded so serious, Marguerite, for a minute there I hardly recognized you."

Annie walked in. "Hello, Miss Vivi, Miss Marguerite. I am glad you are able to laugh, but it's gettin' late. You don't want to miss your own weddin' now, do you? Since you won't be comin' back here, I will pack the rest of your things to be sure you don't lose anythin'."

"Thanks, Annie, and I want the two large suitcases and the overnight bag left in the car."

"You mean you are goin' on a honeymoon?"

"Yes, Annie."

"Mr. Ben is a man after my own heart. He sure knows a lady when he sees one. I tell you, Miss Vivi, you are in good hands. He will be good to you, because if he makes any mistakes, he has me to answer to, plus a couple of friends you don't even know you have."

Vivi was touched by the older woman's sincerity and loyalty, and was about to thank her when she said, "There's no need to get maudlin now. The worst is over. This is the good part. Come, let me help you, child. But don't you put that dress on yet. A bride is suppose to be late, and you are not goin' to be any different." With a wink she said, "I've been savin' this for a special occasion and I can't think of anythin' more special than this." She produced a bottle of wine and some cheese and crackers with caviar neatly hidden between. "Now eat this, and let us drink a toast to your future."

"Sorry, Annie, but Vivi doesn't drink alcoholic beverages. I'm just learning to, but now's not the time for this. I'm afraid I might make a mess of things."

"Well!" said Annie. "Wonders never cease. The French stop drinkin' wine?" What will become of all the vineyards in France?"

"I guess they will be shipping all their grapes here from now on!" Vivi said matter-of-factly.

"Annie!" Marguerite scolded. "We can't eat now! We will ruin our makeup."

"And if you don't, you will ruin the weddin'. Now which will it be?"

Obediently they each took a snack and soon discovered they had been hungry.

"Who can eat at a time like this?" Marguerite said between swallows. "Oh, the excitement!"

Vivi was really amazed at the depth of Annie's knowledge and shrewdness, and she held her for a while. "Thank you, Annie, for caring and for being my friend."

The photographers had arrived and were ushered in another room while Annie and Marguerite calmly helped Vivi into her gown as if they had all the time in the world. "Miss Vivi, I don't want you to worry yourself. Stay as calm as you can. Remember this is your weddin'. It can't go on without you. Believe me, I know what I'm doin'. It's hot out there and I don't want you to start sweatin'. That's why I want you to wait till the last minute." Annie was in complete command and Vivi felt better taking orders than having to think for herself.

Her gown was a mass of fine lace over satin, and the train was studded with seed pearls, as was the tiara which held her headdress in place. There also were dozens of teardrops hanging from the headdress, which fell in with the train, causing it to appear as one.

"Oh!" The exclamation escaped as Vivi saw her reflection in the mirror. Annie rushed to her side. "What is it my child?"

"I just wish my mother had lived to see me like this." She knew she couldn't deceive Annie, but she was also entitled to her own thoughts.

Still, that did not explain the look in Annie's eyes when she said, "It's time let me cover your face. People are already gatherin' outside."

***

As Vivi took Ross's arm, she looked as delicate as the pearls about her neck and earlobes. Her satin pumps added the final touch to her ensemble, and she was suddenly assured that Ben would never be disappointed in her appearance.

Annie said, "God bless both of you, Miss Vivi, and when you get to the church, don't bother to look around. Just look for Mr. Ben and everythin' will be all right."

Meanwhile, at the church, Ben was getting worried, He couldn't imagine what was taking Vivi so long. He was beginning to think she changed her mind about marrying him, when the "Wedding March" started to play and everyone stood up.

Slowly she walked down the aisle, and to Ben she seemed to be floating. He wasn't prepared for the vision he saw. She looked like a princess as she handed her bouquet of white orchids to Marguerite and smiled at him. If anyone spoke, he didn't hear. All he could see was the beautiful woman in white who was soon to be his wife.

Once at the altar, when he held her hand, he felt a slight tremor, which heightened his anxiety. He gave her a reassuring smile and, as they exchanged vows, her radiance proved she was happy.

The church was filled, and many lined the streets to have a glimpse of the bride. They took pictures, and she accepted all the congratulations as the various people were presented to her. Though it was evening, the heat was still torrid, but they soon left for home, where the reception was being held. On the way, Ben said, "Congratulations, Mrs. DeVille."

"On what, Mr. DeVille?"

"On becoming my wife."

She kissed him. "You are still the most arrogant man I know, but I love you enough not to start fighting with you already. I also would like to be dressed in something less cumbersome. I can't wait to be home." It suddenly struck her funny that she said home, but that was her home now. She would have to get accustomed to it.

Ben kissed her. "Are you all right, love?"

"Yes. Why?"

"Well, the look I saw on your face a moment ago surely wasn't happiness."

"Ben," she said, "are you going to insist on knowing my every thought?"

"I'm sure going to try, love. In fact, I'm going to make it my business to know every little thing there is to know about you."

Soon after they arrived home, Vivi slipped away and reappeared in a pale blue gown of organza and satin trimmed with a deeper shade blue that emphasized the slimness of her waist and matched the colors of her attendants.

"Oh, there you are, darling. I never knew it was possible for you to look more beautiful than you were a while ago, but you are." He took her arm and led her proudly to the table for the festivities. It was all so wonderful, and when Ben said "On behalf of my wife and myself," she felt as if transported to a place she never dreamed existed.

It was time for them to leave for their honeymoon, and there were the usual rice throwing and cheers as they drove away. Vivi said, "Oh, Ben, I'm so happy. Everything and everyone was perfect. I feel like a princess. I shall never forget this day."

"Neither will I, love. I'm so proud of you, the way you treated the guests as friends, even though you don't know them."

"Thank you. I'm going to do all I can to keep you happy."

Chapter Seven

The Continental Sheraton was almost three hours away by car, and they were exhausted, but Vivi slept while Ben drove, and as he watched her, he thanked his lucky stars that he had the most wonderful woman he had ever known for his wife. He felt a twinge of guilt for not being totally honest with her, but whatever he did in the past had nothing to do with her, he told himself, and seeing he had no intention of betraying her, there was nothing to fear.

Faces loomed at his memory as he tried desperately to forget, but they were real and he knew that they would always be there. If only he had told her before, he could be at peace. This was his honeymoon; he should only be thinking of his wife and the happiness she brought in his life. He thought of waking her and talking to her to blot out the intruders, but he knew she had a long day and needed her rest. She was his wife. The most wonderful thing that ever happened to him was when she agreed to marry him, and he wouldn't let anything or anyone come between them.

Tom Slater, the manager of the hotel, was also a personal friend of Ben's, which had made it quite easy for him to make the arrangements for his honeymoon. He trusted his ability and, above all, his discretion to cover all the necessary areas of his request without him having to go there beforehand. He could hardly wait to see Vivi's reaction when she found out where he was taking her. The first time she saw it, she was so fascinated by it. "Oh! It's beautiful. I hope to spend some time there before I leave," she had said. So much had changed since, and Ben was delighted it all worked in his favor.

He smiled as he looked at her sleeping beside him. He soon reached the little hill a couple of miles from the hotel and he turned off the engine and kissed her gently on the forehead. "Darling, wake up. I have something to show you!"

"What is it?" she whispered with her eyes still closed.

"If you open your eyes, you will see it."

Grudgingly she did, and as she focused, there was instant recognition. "Oh, Ben! You remembered. It seems even more beautiful at night."

"Yes, my love, but not half as beautiful as you."

He held her and kissed her until she felt faint. She knew if she were standing, her knees would give way. Neither of them spoke, and he started the car while she leaned against his shoulder, waiting for him to ameliorate that yet unrevealed stirring she felt at his touch.

They entered the lobby and Vivi noticed a tall man about Ben's age approach with outstretched hands. "Hello, Ben. It's good to see you. Welcome to the Continental."

"Thank you, Tom, and may I present my wife, Vivi."

Slater took her hand and bowed before he kissed it. "Welcome, madame, it's a pleasure to have you here as our guest, and please feel free to call on me personally if there should be a problem."

Ben was watching him intently and said, "Tom, the only problem my wife is going to have is me, and she won't need your help with me, I assure you. Now if you don't mind, will you direct us to our suite?"

"Yes, sir," Tom said with a mock salute, and they all laughed as they took the elevator up. Slater opened the door, and with a flourishing gesture said, "Here we are. I sincerely hope everything is to your liking, madame, and congratulations. Have a wonderful honeymoon."

Vivi was almost speechless at the loveliness of the suite. It was like a rose garden. There were flowers everywhere and a table with a cold supper of lobster, cheeses and a variety of other foods. There was also a fruit basket containing all the tropical fruits she could think of and a bottle of champagne in a cooler. Ben saw that she was pleased and without a word, he picked her up and carried her into the bedroom and laid her gently on the bed.

As he enfolded her in his arms, she felt the tears burning her eyes and wondered why she was crying. She felt so safe with Ben and she was really happy. But somehow she felt the need to delay the moment, and she ran for the bathroom, where she had a bath and hoped that the soothing water would in some way help to obliterate her fears.

At last she decided that there was only one way to find out, and she dressed in a beautiful white negligee and stood in the doorway. Ben must have sensed her presence rather than seeing her, when he looked up and slowly rose to his feet. "Oh, my love! You are like a vision." He held her and allowed all his pent up desire to engulf them both, but he didn't want to rush her. "Darling, why don't we have a drink of that lovely champagne and relax a bit."

"Oh, Ben, I'm beginning to think that's a good idea, but you know I don't drink."

She walked over to the window and gazed out to the ocean where the clamorous waves tossed and splashed at will in the faint moonlight.

It was then she realized that she, too, was free. Like the waves, she was free to love her husband and there was no need for stimulants. A surge of excitement coursed through her entire body, and when she remembered how long she had waited for that day, all her misgivings disappeared.

***

Vivi awoke the next morning to find her husband smiling at her, and said. "Hi, lover. What are you doing, watching me sleep?"

"Not really." He kissed her. "I'm waiting for you to wake up."

"Why?"

"Don't ask."

He drew her closer to him, and knowingly, she said, "Next time you wake me. I have a lot of catching up to do."

***

They dined in their suite and left it only for an afternoon swim. Vivi was fascinated with the ease and friendliness of the people she met, and the deep blue of the ocean against the cloudless sky made it all seem so wonderful to her. She was truly happy, and she could tell Ben felt the same.

On the third day, Ben said, "Would you like to go out tonight, love? Maybe it's time we join the rest of the human race."

"Tired of me already, Mr. DeVille?"

"Not a chance. If you don't feel like it, we'll just find something to do indoors. But I was surely looking forward to showing you off to those poor, unfortunate devils out there."

"Okay, I will go with you on one condition."

"What's that, may I ask?"

"That I will be able to show you off to those poor, miserable women out there."

"Darling, you've got a deal."

"Now what shall I wear?"

He kissed her. "I'm sure you will think of something, but if you prefer, I could help you make up your mind."

Not knowing her wardrobe, he wondered as to whether she had brought appropriate things for what he had planned, but he didn't want to spoil the surprise. "Come, love, let's see what we can do about tonight." Then he saw something green and gave her a wide grin.

"What's so funny?" she demanded, feeling a little foolish.

"Nothing really. I just hope that green dress will keep at least some of you hidden."

"Ben DeVille! It does too. Do you want to see it on?"

"Darling, you know I'd rather you without anything on, but just this once."

She gave him an alluring look and slipped into the dress, then turned for him to do the zipper. Hence, she did not see the hint of surprise in his eyes. When she did discover a note of sadness in his voice, she thought he just didn't like it, although she couldn't imagine why. He turned her around and said, "You are full of surprises, my dear. You look perfect."

"Ben! This is not just any old dress. I couldn't wear it just to sit around. I would look ridiculous."

"Trust me, love, you will be fine, and you stay right there. Don't take it off. I'll be right back."

She started to put her hair in a French roll, wondering if the heat would affect her if she let it fall, when Ben returned. "Here, this is my wedding present to you." In his hand he held a package, and she hesitated for a moment, then opened it.

She gasped, "Oh, Ben, it's so beautiful, but how did you know?"

"Let's just say it's karma, because it surely isn't knowledge."

The emerald and diamond necklace had a matching pair of earrings, and he helped her to put them on. With the pale green of her dress and the color of her eyes, she was so beautiful he could think of only one other person that would look like that. "Vivi, these were my mother's. She left them with a letter for me in Annie's care. 'Son,' she said, 'this is for your wife. Love her and be kind to her. But don't be hasty — wait until you find the right girl.' Then one day Marguerite sent me a picture of you, and somehow I knew you were the one. It is all so funny at times, because you even look like Mother. You were born the same month, and that threw me for a while, but I am not a believer in reincarnation or I couldn't marry you."

She held him to her. "Thanks for telling me all this, and I'm truly honored that you chose me to give this treasure to and to share your life with. I hope wherever she is, she will be able to know how proud I am of you. And now it's my turn. This is for you. It's the key to my father's safety deposit box, the contents of which are yours."

"And where is this box?" he teased.

"Oh, it's at a bank in New York."

"You are a very funny lady."

That night as they dressed, Vivi thought she would humor her husband and do whatever he wanted, although she would hate to seem pompous. "Oh, darling," Ben said, "you look wonderful and I can't wait for you to see what I have planned for us tonight."

"Ben DeVille," she whispered, but before she could say another word, he silenced her with a kiss, then guided her to the elevator.

Once in the lobby, they headed for the ballroom, and as they entered, there was a drum roll and an announcement was made: "Here they are, Mr. and Mrs. Ben DeVille!" There was a band and at least a hundred people all cheering as Vivi stood and gazed in amazement. Soon there was music and, to her surprise, they were playing their song, "Your Precious Love." Ben saw the many questions on her face and took her in his arms, and she lost herself in her newfound happiness.

She had no idea how long she was dancing, but the band had stopped and there were people all around them congratulating them. Vivi felt like a celebrity, having all her needs met and people serving her everywhere. She never dreamed loving another person could be so rewarding. "Oh, Ben," she said, "I can't tell you how happy you've made me. I want to be all you expect me to be, but most of all, I want to be the mother of your children."

She thought she saw a shadow cross his brow, but he just grinned and said, "If you promise me there will be daughters to look just like you."

***

On their return home, they were greeted by Marguerite, who couldn't wait to hear Vivi's account of what happened.

"Oh, Marguerite, I feel as if I owe you my life. I'm so happy that I cannot explain it to you. All I can do is wish for you to have someone to share your life and make you experience the joy of love when it is shared."

They hugged each other as Marguerite said, "Now I am going to try to persuade the Mademoiselle Cupid to find me my prince, but first I must leave and allow you to get on with your life."

"Marguerite," Vivi said, "why so soon? I was hoping you would stay a while and help me settle in."

"*Cherie*," Marguerite took her hand, "for what you have to do now, you need no help, and if you did, it wouldn't be mine."

As Vivi blushed, Marguerite said, "It is okay, *cherie*. You are a woman now, and you have responsibilities. No matter what happens, remember your vows. I love my cousin, but I love you more. You are like a sister to me. I would hate to hear you have done anything foolish. Ben married you because he loves you, and don't you ever forget that. I have to finish packing. I must go, *cherie*, but I will visit you as often as I can."

"Promise?"

"Promise."

Vivi stood rooted to the spot where Marguerite left her, and the more she thought about it, the more she felt that she was being warned of some lurking danger. Ben was watching her and saw that she was deep in thought. He wondered what Marguerite could have said to her to cause such a change in her. "There you are, darling," he said. "Where is Marguerite? I thought you two were together."

"Yes," she said as she gazed into his eyes for some sign, but not knowing what she was looking for, she held him to her and said, "Ben, she told me she will be leaving tomorrow, but there was something else she didn't say."

"What?"

"Ben, I didn't imagine it. There was something in her voice that made me think she was warning me against something."

"Mrs. DeVille, you cannot allow yourself to start imagining things now that you have a husband to take care of."

They both laughed and she followed him into the bedroom, where he made all her doubts disappear.

After Marguerite's departure, Vivi busied herself in her new home, and soon there was evidence of her special touch all around the house. Annie, sensing the need in her new mistress to assert herself, gave her all the support and encouragement she could. She was happy to know that she could teach her mistress something, and one day Vivi got an idea. "Annie," she said, "you know what? I think together we should compile all these beautiful recipes into a cookbook."

She couldn't wait for Ben to come home to tell him the good news, and after he stopped laughing he said, "I'm sorry, but I just can't understand you. Why would you want to go through all that trouble?"

"Because, silly, there is not much else to do around here, and all this food really fascinates me."

"Darling, have I been neglecting you? I thought by now we would be ready to hire a nurse, but in time I hope to keep you so busy that you will lose interest in everything else."

"Ben, I saw the doctor the other day and he said there is no apparent reason that I shouldn't become pregnant. He suggested that we relax and stop thinking about it; then, when we least expect it, we will be successful."

"Sounds like good advice to me, but he forgot one thing. There is no easy way to stop thinking about something as important as that. Oh, I almost forgot. You remember saying you didn't like the horse you were riding the other day? Well, come with me. I have something to show you."

She followed him to the stables, and there was the most beautiful colt she had ever seen, sleek and black as night. "Oh, Ben, I love it."

"Good. She's yours. You have to train her your way, do whatever you like with her, but first you have to name her."

"Ben DeVille, you are the most thoughtful husband any woman could have and I love you for it."

He held her close. "Tell me what else you like about me."

"Well," she hesitated, then whispered in his ear, "everything."

She soon started struggling as if to come up for air and she said, "I know, I am going to call her Jade."

"Darling," Ben said, "kiss me again. I think I've missed something somewhere along the line."

She kissed him, then said, "The colt, silly. I am going to call her Jade."

Ben looked at his wife. She seemed more beautiful every day, but he just couldn't imagine what went on in her head. He said, "Before we leave here my love, would you tell me why you would look on a jet-black colt and call her Jade?"

"The answer to that is very simple, dear. Because I want to."

She ran back to the house and he chased her, but she had anticipated his move, so she got there ahead of him. As Annie watched them together, she felt a happiness she couldn't explain, except that it was good to see two people so much in love. In my opinion, those two were made for each other, she thought.

They had been married for over a year and their time together seemed to be one long honeymoon. They spent most of their time together.

With all the plans for her book, Vivi decided to spend some time in the kitchen to watch as well as help in the preparation of the meals. She was determined to have a firsthand knowledge of whatever she was going to put in print, and the more her interest grew, the more time she spent in the kitchen.

She soon discovered that a lot of people came in and out through the day, but considering the size of the estate and its different functions, she never asked who they were. Some of them were children, and one day, Vivi saw a little boy and she stopped as if planted where she stood. The child was the image of her husband, but if Ben had fathered a child, surely he would have told her. Fascinated by her culinary experiences she soon forgot the child and lost herself in her project.

Annie, being the keen observer, saw the recognition on her mistress's face and wondered why she never mentioned anything that would betray the fact that she knew. This is a real lady, she thought, and Mr. Ben is surely the luckiest man in the world. I can't wait for her to have some of her own.

Ben noticed that Vivi was sleeping a little more than was customary, but seeing she was so active with the training of Jade and her book, he thought she was just tired. Now it was time for their early morning swim, but she didn't budge. "Vivi," he said, nibbling her ear, "let's go."

She moaned unintelligibly and turned on her side. Ben felt like letting her rest, but he knew she would be disappointed, so he insisted that she wake up, and she did. "I am so sorry, Ben. We must hurry. I have a lot to do today."

"Honey, I think you are a bit overworked as it is. What would you say to spending the rest of the day with me? I can take the day off and we can sleep all day or do whatever you like."

Without answering, she got out of bed, slipped into her suit, and headed for the door, with him in tow. "I will give you my answer later, but right now try and catch me." In what seemed like seconds later she was lying on the ground, screaming, "Oh, Ben! Something has happened!"

He ran to her and held her, but her screams were piercing. "Don't touch me. It hurts." Her whole body had become a mass of pain and there was nothing he could do to help her. He tried to pick her up, but her cries hindered him until he realized he had to. She needed a doctor, and the only way to get her there was to pick her up. He took her to the house and called Ross "Ross, Vivi is sick. Drive us to the hospital."

"What happened?"

"I don't know. We were running to the beach when suddenly she fell to the ground screaming."

She was still crying and tossing when Annie came in. "Oh, Mr. Ben," she said, "I think I know what's wrong with her. Hurry to the hospital or she won't make it."

For the second time in years, Ben thought about God in a prayerful way. What did Annie mean when she said she might not make it?

***

The car swerved and she screamed while Ben cradled her head in his arms. What would he do if anything happened to her? He really didn't want to think about that, and thank God they were finally at the hospital.

Doctor Mariel took one look at her and said, "Nurse, prepare her for surgery. It looks like an ectopic pregnancy."

Ben was shocked. "Vivi, you never told me you were pregnant."

"I didn't know," she sobbed as she was wheeled away.

Ben was frantic. "What does that mean, Doctor? Is she going to lose it?"

"Well, if my diagnosis is correct, we will have to move fast or we will lose her. Walk with me, Mr. DeVille. I have to go to her, but in a nutshell, what has happened is that the fetus is developing in the tube instead of the uterus. Don't worry, we will do everything we can. . . ."

"Doctor!" a nurse yelled. "We are losing her. She has lost consciousness."

Dr. Mariel rushed off and Ben stood there with the tears running down his cheeks. "Oh, Vivi, what have I done to you?"

Ross took him to the waiting room and they waited.

A nurse came to them. "Mr. DeVille, your wife has lost a lot of blood. If you care to donate some of yours on her behalf we would greatly appreciate it."

"Oh, nurse, I would gladly give up my life if it would save hers."

Ross was on his feet. "Nurse, you can have two pints of mine if it will help."

"Okay, both of you please follow me. I will have to ask you a few questions concerning your recent health, then we will take it from there."

Ben said, "It's all my fault. If I hadn't made her pregnant, she wouldn't have to go through all this. I will never be able to live with myself if anything happens to her."

Nurse Wiley, knowing who Ben was, said, "Mr. DeVille, this is no time for recriminations. These things do happen to people in all walks of life." The hint of sarcasm did not go undetected, and Ben tried to remember where he had seen her before, but he had no intention of playing her game; his wife's life was on the line and that was all he cared about then. He wished they were able to give her his blood directly, which would make them even more a part of each other.

As he paced the floor, Ross joined him and they clung to each other in silence, each saying a prayer for her and giving support to the other. Ross loved Vivi as he would a sister, and since Ben had married her, she brought so much happiness to the household that even he felt proud of her. "Ben," he said, "I know how much this child must have meant to you, but she will have others."

"I don't care about the child, Ross. No, I didn't mean that. I meant, what if Vivi dies? I couldn't go on living without her. Ross, she's the best thing that ever happened to me, I can't lose her."

"You won't, Ben. You love each other too much and you are a good man. Think positive. We must if she's to pull through."

The door opened and Dr. Mariel said, "Mr. DeVille, your wife is fine, but she is heavily sedated and won't be awake for several hours."

"Thank you, Doctor. May I see her?"

"Yes, of course, but I think you would like to know that luckily there was no damage done. There is no reason why she shouldn't be able to conceive again."

Ben walked into the room and bent over to kiss the almost-still form in the bed. How many times in the past did he wake up and watch her sleeping beside him? And to think he almost lost her! He took her hand and pressed it to his lips. She stirred and moaned. "Ben," she whispered, "I'm sorry."

She wasn't really awake, but he stayed with her and wished he could take away the pain each time she groaned. She called his name constantly and he answered, although he wasn't sure she heard. He told her how much he loved her and even promised never to make her go through that again. He sat with her until Nurse Wiley came in to see if she was awake. "Mr. DeVille," she said, "would you please wait outside? It's time for the patient to be awake, and since she isn't, I'll have to do it."

"Nurse, the patient you refer to happens to be my wife. Are you saying I can't watch while she wakes up?"

"Sorry, sir, but there are rules that have to be enforced, and if I break them for you, I would be expected to do the same for everyone."

"Nurse Wiley," Ben said, looking her straight in the eyes, "if the circumstances were different, I would personally oblige you by brushing that chip off your lovely shoulders, but as you well know, this is neither the time nor the place."

As she gazed back at him, he remembered how well he knew her, but that was a long time ago. Now he was a different man.

She checked the IV and said, "Mrs. DeVille, it's time to get up. Can you hear me? Your husband is here to see you."

"Ben," she said and winced as she tried to move. "I lost our baby, so sorry."

"Oh, darling, I'm here. Don't worry about the baby. Now you need to get well. Then we can discuss that."

"If only I had known, I would have taken better care of myself." She tried to open her eyes, but only the teardrops escaped, and Ben wiped them away. He then broke down and cried, not caring if she heard him, but it was quite evident that he would never be able to tell her, now that she didn't have her baby. He cried for her, but mostly for himself, his lack of courage, his weakness that prevented him from being honest with her.

Lord Byron's words reverberated in his mind with such force, he turned and looked, but there was no one there. It had come from within.

The thorns which I have reap'd are
of the tree I planted
They have torn me and I bleed
I should have known what fruit
Would spring from such a seed.

Words of accusation, he had become fair game for condemnation, even from one so long dead, but he deserved it.

Chapter Eight

At the mention of Ben's name, Vivi broke down. "I have failed him, Annie," she cried. "I have lost our baby. He is going to hate me. What if he thinks I didn't want to have children? Oh, Annie, I just didn't know I was pregnant. There were no signs."

"Miss Vivi," Annie said, "Mr. Ben loves you and I know he would want a lawful heir, but he loves you for yourself, and after all, even if he never gets a child by you, he has the others. Believe me, all you got to do is get well and come home."

Vivi's eyes flew open, but Annie was so caught up in her effort to console her mistress, by the time she noticed her expression, it was too late. Poor Annie had the answer to the most puzzling question she had debated for so long. She never acknowledged the children because she never knew they existed. How could Mr. Ben do that to such an innocent and trusting girl?

Vivi became hysterical, and Annie summoned the doctor, who gave her a sedative, then took Annie aside. "Annie, I understand you were with Mrs. DeVille. Can you tell me what brought that on?"

"No, Doctor," Annie lied. "We were talking about the baby she lost when she suddenly fell apart."

"Thank you, Annie, you can go home now. She will be sleeping for a while, but ask Mr. DeVille to stop by my office whenever he comes in."

Dr. Mariel always thought of himself as a good judge of character and he knew Annie had lied to him; he just couldn't imagine why. "Nurse Wiley," he said, "see that Mrs. DeVille has no visitors." He turned to leave, then added, "Oh, and please ask her husband to see me when he gets back."

Annie knocked, and the voice on the other side of the door said, "Come in." As she looked at the broken man lying on the bed, her anger slowly dissipated and was replaced by pity.

"How is she, Annie?" Ben asked in a strangely hushed voice.

"She's worse, Mr. Ben. She was talkin' and I was tryin' to console her when it happened."

"When what happened?" he yelled.

"Well, she became hysterical, Mr. Ben, and Lord, the look in her eyes will go with me to my grave."

"What look, Anne? What did you say to her?"

"It is all my fault. If anythin' happens to her I will never forgive myself."

"Damn it, Annie. What the hell are you talking about?"

"She said you would hate her for losin' the baby and I told her no, but she was cryin' and I said even if she didn't have any of her own, you have the others."

"What?" Ben screamed. "You told her about . . . ?"

"I didn't know you didn't tell her, and she's seein' them every day. How could she not know?"

"Oh, my God, Annie, I've got to see her and beg her forgiveness. Believe me, Annie, I wanted to tell her but was afraid of losing her if I told her before we were married. Then afterwards, I just couldn't find the right time. I know that's deception, but we were so happy. I . . . I didn't want that to come between us. There were times when I wished she would find out, but not like this, not when her life depends on it."

"Mr. Ben, you are like a son to me, and I am very sorry you are in this mess, but you caused it all on yourself. Why didn't you trust her enough to tell her?"

"Annie, if I knew the answer to that, there would be no need for this discussion. I'm going to see her."

***

Dr. Mariel knew something quite traumatic had taken place to cause such a drastic change in his patient's condition. For two days she seldom opened her eyes, and medically there was no cause for her reaction. "Mrs. DeVille," he said as he took her pulse and found it normal, "how are you today?"

"Why don't you tell me? You are the doctor."

"Good. I see you are feeling better. Now I'll let your husband see you for a few minutes."

When she didn't react to the mention of her husband, Dr. Mariel knew he was on the right track. Then, when Ben walked in and her countenance changed, his suspicions were confirmed.

Not caring whether she could hear him or not, Ben knelt by her bed and called her. "Vivi," he said, "I know I was wrong not to tell you, but I'm leaving it up to you to decide our future. I don't know if you can find it in your heart to forgive me, but I was so afraid of losing you that I kept putting it off for tomorrow, until it got too late. There were times when I thought you knew but just refused to discuss it. I know it's painful for you, but a part of me is relieved. At least I don't have to walk around with the guilt anymore. Oh, Vivi, my darling, I love you. Don't turn your back on me now, I beg of you. Please understand that I was trying to protect you. It wasn't a plan to deceive you."

For the first time, she spoke, and there was no mistaking the venom in her voice. "Love, Ben? You say you love me when all this time you have lied to me?"

"Vivi, it was an omission. You never asked, and I didn't have the guts to tell you."

"I don't want to see you when I leave here. You don't have to worry, I will move into a hotel."

"Vivi, I know I was wrong and you are disappointed in me, but please don't make any hasty decisions. Get well and then we can discuss this rationally."

"The time for discussion is past, Ben. Now will you please leave?"

"Okay, Vivi. I will leave, but I will be back tomorrow."

"No!" she said a little too loudly, and wondered, of the pain in her heart and the one from the incision, which was greater.

Dr. Mariel was not acquainted with Ben DeVille personally, but his reputation had preceded him. He was said to have been the Casanova in those parts, and he had the wealth to maintain it. How could he be so lucky to have a woman like Vivi, he wondered, and where did she come from? Since the first time he had seen her, he couldn't seem to think of anyone else. If that womanizer ever did anything to hurt her, he would personally get him for it. What am I saying? he said to himself as he paced the floor of his small office. She's my patient! It's also time to make my rounds.

"*Comment allez vous, mademoiselle?*" he said as he entered her room.

"I'm fine, Doctor," she replied in English.

The sight of her lying there sent his heart racing. She looked so helpless, he wished he could hold her in his arms and make everything all right. While taking her pulse, he was aware of the sensation he felt by touching her, but so as not to alarm her, he said, "I'm glad you're feeling better. In fact, you should have been up and about days ago. You must get out of bed, Mrs. DeVille, or the pain won't go away."

She opened her eyes and he smiled tenderly at her, then said, "That's better. I have been meaning to speak to you about your relapse. You did lose a lot of blood when your husband brought you in, but you were doing very well after surgery. Would you care to tell me what your housekeeper did to make you seem to lose the will to live?"

Vivi turned away from him, but she didn't reply.

"Very well, I'm sorry to pry, but if there is anything I can do, please let me know. One more thing — I will send a nurse to get you out of bed. Please be nice to her, and if you are worrying about having children, you can. Just concentrate on getting well and being home with your family."

"Home, Doctor? There are times when I wonder where is home."

"Well, my lady, if the proverb is correct, that's where the heart is."

"Doctor, the problem is, I don't know anything anymore."

The more she spoke, the more his fascination grew. Her accent was strangely beautiful, and there was a certain quality about her. He was gazing at her and she said, "Don't tell me I look that terrible. You looked as if you saw a ghost."

"I'm so sorry. I can explain. You reminded me of someone I used to know," he lied as he left the room.

At the nurses' station, Dr. Mariel said, "Nurse Wiley, I want you to go to Mrs. DeVille's room and see that she walks around a bit."

"Yes, Doctor, and her husband is here to see you."

"Tell him I'll see him in ten minutes."

Dr. Mariel took one look at Ben DeVille, and the only thing he felt for him was disgust. "What is the matter, Ben? Oh, I'm sorry, may I call you Ben?"

"Yes, of course, Doctor," Ben replied with suppressed anxiety.

"Well, what can you tell me about your wife's refusal to see you? I take it that's why you are here."

"Yes. There are things about me that I should have told her long ago, before I married her, and somehow, out of fear of rejection I kept putting it off. The other day Annie, our housekeeper, let it slip." He got up and walked toward the window. "How long have you worked here, Doctor?"

"Well, just about three years."

"I see." There was a moment of complete silence, then Ben screamed, "I'm not proud of what I've done, but that's the way it was before I met her."

"What are you saying, Ben? The way what was?" he coaxed.

"Well, there were lots of women, but I swear to you since I first saw her picture, I gave them all up. We were pen pals, you know? Me writing to a woman."

Dr. Mariel knew there was more, and he waited, lightly tapping a pencil on his desk as he watched the wretched creature before him squirm.

"You don't understand, Doctor. There were children."

"What? And how did she take it when you told her?"

"Don't you see? I didn't tell her," he whispered. "I just couldn't. I never meant to hurt her. I guess I loved her too much. I had to protect her."

"I see," said Dr. Mariel. "Do you care to tell me how many children there are?"

"Five."

"Well, Ben, pardon me for being so blunt, but you are a fool, and you almost caused her irrevocable damage. I am going to have a little talk with her, but if she insists on your staying away from her, I expect you to respect her wishes. Also, I want you to bear this in mind. I cannot think of one reason to help you. I will be doing this for my patient."

"Thank you, Doctor. I appreciate it anyway," Ben said, extending his hand, which Dr. Mariel ignored, and walked out.

He watched Ben leave, then he returned to his office and closed the door as he sat down heavily in his chair. Ben DeVille did not deserve a woman like Vivi, but she was his wife. Oh God, he thought as he gazed out the window, I'm in love with her. How can I help her without helping that bastard as well? Why did I allow this to happen? She's my patient, for goodness sake. The only decent thing to do is to remove myself from her case. I'll ask Dr. Frank to take over for me.

Not knowing what to do, he got up and opened the door, and there she was, holding on to her nurse, in a pale pink gown with ribbons of a brighter shade that seem to flow all around her. Her hair hung loosely about her shoulders and her eyes looked as if she was oblivious to her surroundings. Even then she was beautiful, and without thinking, Dr. Mariel went to the nurses' station and took a single rose from the arrangement. "Here, Mrs. DeVille," he said, "will you accept this as a reward for the progress you've made?"

She hesitated, then reached for it with her free hand. "Thank you, Doctor, but I hope you will forgive me if I am not able to meet your expectations."

"Nurse, do you mind leaving us for a while? I need to speak with Mrs. DeVille." He took her arm and started back in the direction of her room, wondering what to say to her, but he was also acutely aware of her perfume and the warmth of her body.

"So, what did you have to discuss with me, Doctor?"

"First, Mrs. DeVille, your attitude. I am aware that you have had a terrible shock, but why are you so hard on yourself? You will be able to lead a normal life, but first you have to concentrate on getting well. Please forget everything else for a while, and feel free to let me know if there is anything I can do to help. That is my only purpose in life, to help."

They were back in her room and he helped her into bed, when suddenly she burst into tears. "Oh, Doctor, how could I be such a fool? Everybody in town must be laughing at me. And do you know who is the cause of it? My husband. Maybe losing this baby was the best thing that ever happened to me. Can't you see I didn't even know I was pregnant? What must he think of me compared to the mother of his children?"

"You are upset and understandably so. Let it all out, and you will feel better."

She buried her face in his chest and cried until there were no more tears, not noticing the broken figure at the door who longed to dry them.

The moments were stolen, but they were his. He held her in his arms as he had wished so often before, but he had to do the right thing. He must be honest with her and hope for the best. "Mrs. DeVille, it is a pity that your husband used poor judgement by not telling you before, but I think he's a decent man. He came to me earlier and explained what had happened, and inasmuch as I disagree with his method, I understand when he said he was afraid of losing you. He loves you and wants to explain the whole rotten business, but you have to give him a chance. See him, at least, or I'm afraid he might do something drastic."

Her body tensed, and realizing he had struck a nerve, he continued. "You shouldn't be too hard on him. He is only a man, and as for your pregnancy, no one can be

blamed for that. These things do happen. Now you must rest. I think I will prescribe a sedative for you tonight."

"Thank you, Doctor, but that won't be necessary. I need to think what I'm going to do with the rest of my life."

"One more thing, Mrs. DeVille. Take my advice. Try not to dwell on the past so much. If you do, you will suffer needlessly and delay your recovery."

"Thanks for listening to me, Doctor, and I do apologize for my behavior. It was very wrong of me to involve you in my personal problems."

"Think nothing of it, my lady. As your doctor, my duty is to make you well in whatever way I can."

Once in his office, Dr. Mariel washed his hands and reached for a towel when the door suddenly opened and Ben DeVille entered. He took one look at him and his worst fears became reality. They stood and stared at each other till Ben said, "Does she know you are in love with her, Doctor?"

"Oh, no. I promise you she never will, but there is no use denying it any longer. I don't even know how it happened, but I will ask you one small favor, if I may. Take care of her. She reminds me of the sunshine in my country on a cold day, bright and beautiful, but powerless to penetrate its surroundings. You are a lucky man, Ben. How often do you find one woman with beauty, intelligence, grace and –"

"Excuse me, Doctor, but I'm delightfully cognizant of my wife's attributes and can assure you there is more to her than one stolen embrace. I'll tell you something else. What you're doing is unethical, and if you ever try to influence her in any way, it will also prove to be rather unhealthy for you. I warn you, Mariel, keep your hands off my wife."

Chapter Nine

On his way home from the hospital, Ben pondered the events that led to that moment in his life, and wished with all his heart he could change them. He never did care for a place in society, as it were, mostly because of his late father. Knowing he had plundered his way to his fortune by taking whatever he wanted and still holding his station, Ben thought it all a game, and he refused to have anything to do with it. His father was cruel and selfish, even to his mother, and he promised himself not to be like him in any way. Yet, now he could see that he wasn't exactly honest in his dealings with women either. His mind drifted, and he remembered how beautiful his mother was, and he still silently grieved for her at times, wondering why she had left him so soon.

But now there was Vivi — the only reason he had changed his ways. Never in his life did he expect to meet anyone like her, but for some unknown reason, he was given a second chance. There were some things that couldn't be changed, but he vowed that nothing was going to stand in his way of happiness. He was setting the stage for his bride-to-be, and would live like the gentleman he was. With a fresh burst of confidence then, he had promised Ross that he would be honest with her whenever he met her, and then let her decide.

Ross had remarked on all the rotten things he had done and thought it very noble of him to be willing to tell all to a virtual stranger. One thing he was sure of, even then, was that he loved her and was therefore willing to make the necessary sacrifices, knowing instinctively it would all be worth it.

How well he remembered the terror he felt when Ross mentioned his various offspring, as he called them. He loved them, but he loved Vivi too, and he was sure they could all co-exist. They could be step-children in name only, but he would not ask her to have any form of involvement in their lives. They had their mothers; he wasn't going to let anyone ruin this for him.

Their faces seemed to burn in his memory: Kevin, twelve years, Craig, ten, and Anthony was about seven. Then the girls: Monica was five, and little Dosia was only three. She was his favorite. It wasn't as if he didn't provide for them. He would have to speak to their mothers regarding his plans and let them know he wouldn't be coming around anymore. And the ones on the estate, he would find homes for them elsewhere. Having five children with five different women was a feat accomplished only by the "village ram" and he knew it. The only difference was they were not all in the same parish. He believed the two on the estate would pose a bit of a problem, but the minute she agreed to marry him he would explain it all to her and allow her to decide, If she truly loved him, she would understand.

However, when he finally met her and saw how innocent she was, he just had to protect her from the world he had lived in for so long. Mostly he wanted nothing more than to be with her. He was awed by her brilliance while intrigued by her naivete. And he knew then that he had finally found a woman with whom he could be happy. If she would have him, he pledged to use that opportunity to redeem himself from all the hurt he had caused her predecessors. His whole attitude changed, he felt like a new man and he was grateful to her for her redemptive ability.

He sighed as he remembered how much he tried to tell her of his past indiscretions, but fear of losing her outweighed good judgement. Because of his old ways, he had made a lot of enemies among men his age, and if he had slipped, they would use her to get even with him. Consequently, he never let her out of his sight for long. She was afraid to drive, saying the roads were too winding and narrow. Therefore, he had the pleasure of taking her wherever she went. He was so proud to be seen with her; how could he hurt her so?

Then came the day when Annie said, "Mr. Ben, when are you goin to marry that nice little lady and settle down?"

He could still remember the pounding of his heart. "Thank you, Annie. I have always trusted your judgment."

But later that day, Vivi had sprained her ankle and they had a terrible fight which ended with him walking out on her. He was hurt by her actions, but staying away from her was even more painful, and later that night he went to see her and asked her to marry him. That was the happiest day in his life when she said yes, but now due to his stupidity, she might leave him. He couldn't go on if it came to that. He must do whatever it took to regain her trust, but where would he start? How does one deal with matters of the heart?

Never before did he see himself as a coward, but his actions proved him to be spineless, and even if she recovered and found it in her heart to forgive him, he would always hate himself for what he had done to her. The pain in his heart intensified, and though it was almost midnight he refused to turn on the lights, not wanting to see the empty space beside him. How he missed her, but she refused to see him. Earlier he had tried, but the nurse informed him that she should have no visitors. "No visitors!" he had said. "I am her husband."

"It's the doctor's order, sir."

That sanctimonious wretch of a nurse. Even she was reveling in his misery, as if it was all his fault. Then it struck him: it was his fault. He was the one who made her pregnant. Why couldn't this have happened to any of the other women? They never even wanted children. "Oh, my God," he cried, as shame and disgust took hold of him. How could he even think such a thing? He must be losing his mind.

As he drifted in and out of sleep, he dreamed he saw her drowning, but all his efforts to save her were futile and he woke up screaming, "Vivi, don't leave me."

Afraid to go back to sleep, he sat in a chair, but he dozed off and soon his mother was standing before him saying, "How could you, Ben?"

"It was an accident, Mother," he replied.

But she walked away, saying, "She's gone, Ben, gone, gone, gone. . . ."

Springing to his feet, he rushed to the door, but when he looked out, it was still dark. He had to know if she was all right. He got in the car and started the engine, when Ross appeared in the doorway. "Where are you going in such hurry, Ben?" said Ross, out of the shadows.

"I'm going to see Vivi."

"Ben, do you realize what time it is?"

"I don't care! I've got to see her."

Ross was by his side. "If you must go, then I'll drive, but it is four a.m. Just how do you propose to get in?"

"I don't know, Ross, but I had a dream, and I think something is wrong with her."

"It was only a dream, Ben. If anything had happened, don't you think they would have called us?"

"I guess you're right. But I feel so helpless."

"Guilt can destroy a man, Ben, but what happened to Vivi could have happened to anyone. You shouldn't take all the blame. Let's go inside. I'll make us some coffee, and while we're at it, when was the last time you ate?"

"I don't know, but I'm not hungry."

Ross suddenly turned to find Ben staring intently at the portrait of their mother that hung on the adjoining wall of the parlor and said, "I often wonder how there could be such a resemblance between two people. There were times when I thought that was one of the reasons you were so smitten with Vivi, but was afraid to mention it. Then, as I got to know her, I decided whatever your reason for loving her, you were justified."

Meanwhile, Ben was lost in thought. He didn't know enough about his wife, and if he could find one thing to prove she had not been completely honest with him, it might help. "Ross," he said, "Vivi gave me the key to a safety deposit box as a wedding gift, but I've never used it. Now I think it's time."

"Where's this box, Ben?"

"New York."

"Oh, I see."

"Ross, I have always given her excuses why I couldn't leave the estate, and I wanted us to go together, but if this could help me in any way, I am going to try."

"What do you expect to find?"

"I don't know, but I want her to know that I'm going, so she has another chance to level with me if there is anything she's hiding."

Later that morning he called the airline, as well the Plaza Hotel in New York, and made reservations. He then drove to the hospital, but Vivi still refused to see him. He sent her a note to let her know his plans, but although he waited for a reply, none came.

His next stop was Dr. Mariel's office. "I will be out of town for a few days. This is where I can be reached in case my wife needs me."

The good doctor didn't miss the sarcasm in Ben's voice, but he simply said, "Yes."

However, the questioning look on his face told Ben that he was somewhat baffled as to why he would take a trip at that particular time. With a knowing smile and threatening gaze, Ben said, "It's business, doctor. My business." As he walked out the door, he gave Dr. Mariel one last look and slammed the door as hard as he could.

On arriving in New York, he was once more fascinated with its beauty, but he knew that it also had its dark secrets of suffering, sadness and even death. It was late evening. There was nothing he could do anyway. He wandered about aimlessly, hoping to tire himself enough to be able to sleep. People came at him from all directions, and he soon got tired of dodging them and headed back to his hotel.

Feeling completely lost, he got in the shower and let the water cover him as he cried. Giving himself completely to his emotions, he cried for his wife, his mother, himself, and even the many people he had caused pain. As he emptied himself of all his pent up grief, he felt better and earnestly prayed that there was nothing in Vivi's past that could come between them, because he didn't want to live without her.

He must have drifted off for a while, because the next time he looked out the window, there was a sudden burst of crimson light beneath the clouds to hail the arrival of the dawn. He shaved and dressed for breakfast, but it was too early. Not that he would have eaten, but he desperately needed some coffee. He decided he'd go for a walk. Once in the street, he saw people waking up on the pavement while others were still asleep. We all have our problems, he thought. They only come in different forms.

He walked up to Fifth Avenue and turned left on Thirty-fifth, continued over to Eighth and turned back to the hotel. He called Ross through the hotel operator. "Hi, Ross. Is everything all right?"

"I guess so. Annie went to see Vivi and she still refuses to come home. But she's much better. Ben, since she has a private room. Give her some time. I'm sure she'll come around."

"Okay, Ross. I hope to be home tomorrow."

At nine o'clock, Ben went downstairs and hailed a cab. He gave the driver the address.

"That's a Chase Manhattan bank, sir. Is that where you want to go?"

"Yes." He hoped this wasn't going to be one of those drivers who talked non-stop. Luckily, they soon reached the bank, and he paid him and waved him on.

Ben went to the information desk and said, "Hello, I'm Ben DeVille. I would like to get to my safety deposit box."

"Oh," the girl said. "You've got to see the manager, sir. First door to your right."

The door was marked "Tom Bascombe, Manager." Ben greeted him by name, then stated his business.

"Please be seated, Mr. DeVille."

Tom Bascombe was a balding, rather rotund gentleman with eyes that somehow told Ben DeVille that he was expecting him. He shuffled a few pieces of paper, then said, "Mr. DeVille, as you know, there are procedures to this sort of thing. Will you please excuse me while I make a call?"

"Yes, of course."

"You must understand, I must have permission from her attorneys."

"Certainly," said Ben, "and you'll also need these." He handed him his identification.

"Agar and Phipps," said the secretary at the other end. "Oh, Mr. Bascombe, one moment, sir."

She buzzed and Phyllis Phipps said, "Hello, Tom. What can I do for you?"

"Well, Mr. Ben DeVille is here."

"Oh? Let me speak to him. Hello, Mr. DeVille. How's your lovely wife?"

"A bit under the weather, but she'll be fine."

"I know, I spoke to her yesterday. Take good care of her, or you'll answer to me."

"Thank you," he said with a grin, and handed back the phone to Bascombe.

"It's okay," she said. "He can take the contents except the documents."

"You must leave the documents," stressed Bascombe, "but you may have the rest."

"That's fine," Ben said. "I only need to verify a few facts, anyway."

As Tom Bascombe led the way to the vault, Ben wondered what he was really hoping to find, but having reached so far, there was no turning back.

"Here you are, sir," said the plain looking young woman who held the other key. She seemed shy, but Ben was aware that she was looking him over. Ben sat at the table and motioned for her to sit on the opposite side. He carefully examined the contents and soon picked up a single strand of pearls and handed it to her.

"But I couldn't," she protested.

"Of course you can. Wear it well. It becomes you."

She opened her mouth to thank him, but just giggled instead as she secured it in her skirt pocket.

Ben then picked up a pair of cufflinks studded with rubies and diamonds. He smiled and put them in his breast pocket.

There were deeds to several real estate holding, savings account numbers, stocks, bonds and two wills. One of the wills was from Vivi's father, making her his sole heir, and the other left him as sole beneficiary unless she had children.

He felt like a fool. It was quite evident she had trusted him from the very beginning and he only lied to her. He wrote one address on a slip of paper and thanked the young woman for her time and returned the box. Rushing out to the street, he wished he had taken the earrings and necklace set, which he guessed must have belonged to her mother. He was thinking of everything, but nothing told him how to win his wife's trust a second time. So she was wealthy and she never told him, but how terrible could that be? She must be made to understand that he tried to tell her, but the timing was never right.

He had asked Bascombe the volume he handled for Vivi, and he said one or two million. Except — he had stopped him before he said any more.

Now on his way to the address he had copied from one of the documents, he thought aloud, "Imagine, I had the key to this information since we were married. But she could have told me. She made light of her inheritance, which technically amounted to a lie. Saying she was comfortable was an understatement, which could be used to protect herself." The only trouble with it was that it could in no way hurt him, which meant it couldn't be used against her. He would have to be a man and face what he had done regardless of the outcome.

The furniture store was located on one of the fringes of Little Italy in Chinatown, and was so large it occupied an entire block. They carried a wide variety of furnishings from Early American and Victorian to French Provincial and Italian. He located the manager and said, "May I see the owner, please?

"Oh, well, sir, that's impossible. Maybe I can be of service."

"No, I must see the owner."

"But she never comes here!"

"Never?"

"You see, sir, since her father died, she decided to live abroad permanently."

"Oh, I see," said Ben. "I'm sorry to have troubled you, but since I'm here, I'll look around a bit."

Strangely enough, the picture of Van McNeil still hung in its place, naming him as proprietor. On the second floor, he went into a small alcove and there it was. The perfect Victorian-style set comprised of two chairs, a desk, a chaise lounge and two matching lamps. The woodwork was magnificent, in light color, as was the upholstery, of the same hue of brocade with mint green and the most delicate shade of pink. They were perfect.

A timid looking salesman with huge glasses walked up to him and said, "May I help you, sir?"

"Yes. I would like to have the contents of this area."

"You mean all of these, sir?"

"Yes," Ben said, and proceeded to point to each piece as he counted them aloud. "There are six items, but I would also like the matching rug. Do you have it in stock?"

"Oh, yes, sir! These are just the floor samples. We'll give you brand new ones."

"Thank you. Now, will you have them shipped to this address?"

"Sure, sir, and how are you going to pay, sir? Cash or charge?"

They did the paperwork and Ben gave him a check for the amount plus a shipping cost. The salesman looked at his name and rushed to the manager's office. Ben could see they were trying to stop him. He continued outside in feigned ignorance and was instantly lost in the lunch hour crowd.

As he pushed and dodged through the ever growing throng, he finally made it to Canal Street, where he got a taxi. On reaching the hotel, he threw his belongings in a bag, paid his bill and was on his way to Kennedy Airport. He knew his reservation was for the following day, but he went on standby, determined to leave on the first plane going to Jamaica, no matter to which airport it was going.

Several people tried to have conversations with him during the time he waited, but gave up when they noticed that he was in a world of his own. The truth was, he knew it too, and for the first time in his life, admitted to himself that there was something he couldn't fix. He wasn't about to give up without a fight, but it was all in Vivi's hands.

Chapter Ten

The first flight available was the "night flight" to Kingston, but in his desperation he took it, knowing he could rent a car. They landed about three a.m., and after several phone calls, he got a car at about four a.m. He realized that he was tired, for he had not allowed himself to fall asleep on the plane due to the nightmares he'd been having lately. Now he was going to drive almost to the other end of the island alone. But he was going to be the first person his wife saw when she woke up.

The hours seemed to stretch to match the vastness of the land, but he drove on. He would do anything for her, and he couldn't wait to tell her so. Passing through the various townships, he imagined the sleeping occupants of the homes and envied them. Then, on reaching Bog Walk, he was completely enveloped by fog, but he continued.

How many times he had driven on that road before; now somehow it was different. He switched on the radio, and the first song they played was "If I Had a Pair of Wings." As often as he had heard that song before, it never bothered him, but in the early morning it sounded as if its sole purpose was to increase his misery. Still, he kept it on, telling himself he needed it to keep him awake. He drove with renewed vigor, and to occupy his mind he made notes of the historical points on the way, then timed himself how long it should take to reach them. He reached them with precision, and would call out the names as if he were a train conductor.

Somehow, Ben had forgotten the Continental Hotel, where they had spent their honeymoon, but on reaching it, he felt a wave of happiness as he began to relive their time together there.

At eight a.m. he reached the hospital in Westmoreland and was told his wife had been released.

***

The previous day, Ross was up very early. He moved about quietly so Annie wouldn't think she had to get up too. He was going to the hospital to see Vivi. His only problem was, he didn't know if she would see him. On recognizing him, the nurse said, "I'll tell Mrs. DeVille you're here, sir." She returned smiling. "You may go in now, sir. She's waiting for you."

"Hi there," he said, bending to kiss her cheek. "How are you?"

"Oh, Ross, physically I'm fine. It's so good to see you. Dr. Mariel says I can go home."

"Well, that's the best news I've heard in a long time. We miss you so much. This is cause for a celebration."

"No, Ross, I don't think that will be necessary. I plan to stay in a hotel for a while to think things through. There are a few things I need to sort out; then I might go to the apartment in New York."

"But Vivi," said Ross, "we all love you."

"Do you, Ross? Are you telling me that not letting me know the kind of man I was about to marry was 'loving me'? Or didn't any of you think I was capable of making a decision of such magnitude? I should have been told, Ross."

"Yes, but it wasn't our place to tell you, Vivi, and you must remember we love Ben too. He's my brother and the only family I know. Yet, if I thought he would willfully hurt you, I couldn't be held responsible for what I would do to him. I didn't know he was such a coward. We discussed it before you arrived, and he promised me he would tell you. As a matter of fact, it was his idea to tell you so there would be no secrets between you. He does love you, Vivi. You are the most precious person in his life. Without you, there will be no Ben, and I'm not going to sit by idly while you ruin your lives because of his past."

She gave him a quizzical look.

"Yes, Vivi. I know his story, but how about yours? Are you saying you don't love him anymore? There's something you need to know. He's been faithful to you even before he asked you to marry him. I can swear to that. Do you know he's in New York?"

"Yes."

"He called to say he would be returning home today. Will you let him find you there when he comes home?"

"Ross, maybe I married the wrong brother. I never thought you had it in you, the concern for us. I believe you really care. However, I will find it difficult to forget what he did. Please understand, Ross, I will go home, not because of Ben or your kindness to me, but I've made a vow before God and all those people, and I'm going to keep it. Let's go."

Ross went to the nurses' station and picked up the phone. "Annie," he said, "prepare Vivi's room. We're coming home. Don't forget the flowers . . . and have you heard from Ben?"

"No, sir."

"Well, we will have to do what we can."

"Praise be!" Annie said and hung up the phone. Then she panicked. She was the one who had let the proverbial "cat out of the bag." Vivi must hate her. But then Annie wasn't one to spend too much time on recriminations. She said, "I think they should all thank me for doin' somethin' they should have done a long time ago." With that, she put the matter from her mind and was her happy self again.

As Nurse Wiley wheeled Vivi to the car, Dr. Mariel stared out his office window and wondered what he was going to do to fill the void in his heart. He knew there was no chance of him having her, but he had been content with watching over her at nights. Now she was gone. Now she was going home to a husband who didn't even deserve her. How often he thought of keeping her in the hospital on some contrived medical excuse, but he couldn't. His only hope was that she saw the love in his eyes and knew how he felt about her. He had taken the liberty to tell her that if she needed anything she shouldn't hesitate to call him, but she chose to go home to her philandering husband.

Turning away from the window, his eyes fell on the sign on his desk. "DR. JEAN PAUL MARIEL, M.D." What am I doing, he scolded himself. I'm a doctor! He screamed inwardly as he slammed a fist on the desk. I know I'm a doctor! But am I not also a man? There were no answers, he concluded, knowing this was so because the questions weren't being addressed objectively.

When Ben accused him of being in love with his wife, to his surprise, he didn't deny it even though he was aware of the consequences should Ben decide to take action against him. To think he had the gall to admit his indiscretion to Ben, of all people, but at least that might prompt him to take better care of her, knowing he had competition. He told himself that he was going to forget her, so he plunged into his work and vowed to start dating again whenever he had some free time.

Chapter Eleven

When Vivi agreed to go home from the hospital, she did so because she knew it was her duty. She was aware that there were several unanswered questions, but she was determined to deal with them in time. But first she must face the children. How could she be such a fool not to have noticed them? Could it be that Marguerite had found out and was trying to warn her? If Ben really loved her, how could he have lied to her all this time? The questions echoed in her mind as they seemed to collide, crashing against each other, but there were no answers.

Fortunately, she was entering their bedroom, and in her heart she knew that whatever else was wrong in her life, that room was where she belonged. Overcome with love and frustration, she broke down and wept. Annie helped her into bed while she explained what she thought had to be said.

"I apologize for causin' trouble between you and Mr. Ben, Mrs. DeVille. But —."

"Oh, Annie! There's no need for you to apologize. After all, you could be the only honest person in this household. If it weren't for you, I would have continued being the laughingstock of this community. My husband has lied to me, Annie. There is no need for me to blame anyone else for that."

At that moment Ben walked in, and Vivi was shocked at how much he had changed in those few days. Her heart went out to him, but she managed to restrain herself as he approached her and sat on the bed. "Hello," he said. "How are you feeling?"

"Fine," she said.

"I missed you, Vivi! Can we talk?"

"About what, Ben?"

"Us."

"There is no 'us', Ben. There is me, and there is you; no more us – you've seen to that."

"Oh, Vivi, be reasonable! All I did, I did because I couldn't risk losing you."

"So you lied to me? You never thought I would find out eventually? Ben, I trusted you with my very life. What happens to truth and honesty? And all the love you profess to have for me? You lied to me, Ben, and there's nothing you can say that will change that."

"Yes, Vivi, I lied to you. But truth and honesty? That's a laugh. If you are so honest, why didn't you tell me you were a millionaire?"

Vivi felt as if she had been struck. But she recovered quickly and said, "What harm could have come to you by not knowing? I never wanted you to treat me like a rich, spoiled brat. I wanted you to love me for myself and keep you being the head of the household. I never wanted you to think of me as anything other than your wife."

"Well, since I'm not in need, I'm not hurt by your deception, but would you agree that you lied to me?"

"No! That's not the same. That's only an omission. It hasn't taken anything from our relationship."

"Does my past in any way affect our relationship?"

When she didn't reply, he went on. "Vivi, since I met you, we spent almost every day together. Do you think I've been unfaithful to you?"

"I don't know, Ben. I honestly don't know."

"Will you believe me if I tell you that I could never do such a thing to you? I've tried to spare you, as well as myself, the misery of knowing the kind of person I used to be. But I swear to you that's all been over since you came into my life. I love you, Vivi, and always will. Since our skeletons have rolled out of their respective closets, can you please forgive me and let us go on with our lives?"

Ben took her in his arms and said, "Everything about you is beautiful, even your skeleton. Please, Vivi, it's wonderful to hold you again. When I thought I was losing you, it almost drove me crazy. I promise if you'll see it all as a part of my past and my responsibility, you won't be touched by it anymore."

"The children, Ben."

"Yes? What about them? I've been thinking to send the boys to —"

"Not now. I need some time. I'm sorry, but I'd rather not see them for a while. I didn't mean to lose our baby, Ben. It was an accident. I'm sorry I can't measure up to the others."

"Vivi, never let me hear you say anything about measuring up. We have time for children, but if you never have a child, I would still love you more than anyone else in this world."

"Ben, I was so shocked to hear that from Annie, although I think I guessed it a long time ago, but simply went into denial. They look so much like you, a part of me must have known."

"Now that it's all over, I want us to be happy again, Vivi. I hope we can recapture the magic we shared, especially now that I have a rival." He waited for her reaction. "I wonder if I'll be safe with you anymore."

"I'm so glad you noticed," she teased. "He's handsome, French, young and my doctor. You mean he told you?"

"What should he tell me?"

"Did you have a fight with him?"

"Of course not! I only warned him to keep away from you."

"Well, you needn't have bothered. He's no threat to you. I'm a married woman."

They were both tired, and she soon realized he had fallen asleep. She kissed him gently then snuggled closer to him, determined to keep the love they had. Her last conscious thoughts were, even if Ben had a hundred children, I am going to make a hundred and one. After all, he's my husband.

Three days later, Vivi rose at early dawn and began to dress quietly, but Ben was watching her every move. "Do you think you're up to swimming?" he asked.

"Yes," Vivi said, "if you'll go along with me."

Once outside, the cool morning breeze caressed their scantily clad bodies as they slowly walked down the well trodden path. She thought of the last time she had attempted to go swimming and the result of her playfulness. The embryo of a tear was gently whisked away by a gush of wind as reassurance, and in her heart she knew there was no need to worry.

Ben was quiet, and Vivi wished she knew what he was thinking, but from the sensation that emanated from his holding her hand, she felt safe. Once in the water, it soothed not only outwardly but their innermost beings as well, and they were once more lost in each other, forgetting the world and its cares.

Suddenly she began to laugh almost hysterically, and Ben watched her in disbelief. What could be so funny? Finally she said, "Now that you know all about me, what do you think?"

"Oh, I forgot to thank you for the cuff links and all the other things you've given me. And while I was in New York I got you a few things, but that can wait."

"What did you get me?"

"You'll see. I suspect you are gong to continue on your cookbook in a while?"

"Yes. I don't want to sit around. In fact, I think I will begin the moment we get back."

With raised eyebrows Ben said, "Get back from where?"

"I need to finish my sailing lessons. Let's go to Port Royal for a few days."

"Oh, yes," he said with that look in his eyes.

"Sorry to disappoint you," she said, "but for your salacious information, I need my rest. I also need to feel that salt air on my face, which might even help to clear my head."

"My dear, you are the most clear-headed woman I've ever known, and I'd go anywhere with you."

"Let me check our supplies in case I sail away with you."

"How soon can you be ready?"

"Give me an hour."

***

It was October and the rains were beginning. There wasn't much one could do outdoors, and Annie never seemed to leave the kitchen. She always had something for them to taste, and Vivi was herself again. Since they returned from their trip, Ben seldom left the house for more than an hour. It was evident their honeymoon had started all over again.

Being unable to go out, at times the entire household would gather and play games. They taught her to play dominoes and she taught them Scrabble as well as card games. It was wonderful to see that she was not in any way affected by her vast wealth. She was a natural human being.

Annie told them Annancy stories at night as they drank fresh brewed coffee and roasted corn while sitting around the fire. Her favorite story was that of "Jack McGrumma Dandyman" that took at least two hours, depending on what mood Annie was in. It was hilarious and they all had loads of fun. "Life is great for us," she said.

"I would like all the children in these parts to be as happy as I am. Ben, what would you say if I told you I wanted to start an orphanage?"

"Well, that's quite admirable of you, but have you thought it through?"

"Yes, I have, but I need your approval as much as your help."

"Okay, if that's what you want, we'll do it."

When Annie overheard the conversation, she said, "Glory be. I always knew this woman was a saint."

Chapter Twelve

Born in Quebec Canada, Jean Paul Mariel was the only son of Léon and Lucinde Mariel. He was their pride and joy until seven years later, when their little girl, Ouida, came along. Jean Paul was an excellent student and he graduated high school earlier than his peers. He entered college and medical school with the same fervor, and by age twenty-three he had graduated and was ready for internship as a pediatrician. His parents proudly presented him with two tickets to Jamaica. "Oh, Mere!" he said, "thank you and Pere so much. I will call Phillipe and see if he wants to go. Then we can take the girls along."

"Okay, son," said his father. "It's time you have some fun."

Excitedly he called his girlfriend, then Phillipe, and within a week they were on their way, all four of them.

Their tickets were for twenty-one days, but Jean Paul was having so much fun that he decided to stay on. He even convinced the others to stay an extra week, but he was still not ready to return. They left while he began to make plans for a permanent stay. And within a couple of months, he made up his mind he was going to practice medicine there. He called his parents and told them he had decided to apply for internship there.

"What?" said his mother in obvious disbelief.

"Well, Mere," he said, "I like it here and I'm going to give it a try." He knew they would be unhappy for a while; at least it was his decision. He was finally on his own. They would have to accept that he was a man and capable of running his life.

He applied to the Montego Bay Hospital and was accepted, where he would work for seven years as general practitioner. But wanting to specialize in his field, he later transferred to Westmoreland.

There were a few times he thought he was in love, but he was committed to his work and was afraid a wife would interfere with his plans. After making that choice, he played the field and was quite comfortable with his lifestyle until Vivi DeVille came along.

Now he wasn't able to see her anymore, and after his admission to her husband, he dared not call her at home. Frantically, his mind raced on, but he could only see one face, and she belonged to someone else.

The only way to get her was to get rid of her husband. "Oh, what am I saying? God would never forgive me for that, even if I had the guts to do it, and I don't. I'm just a helpless sniveling wimp," he whispered and poured himself another drink. Before all this started, he only drank socially. Now he even stocked the thing at the cottage. "What am I going to do? he yelled as the glass from which he was drinking crashed against the mirror.

In his inebriation, he promised to forget her because that was the right thing to do. "I know what I'll do," he said. "I'll get married. Tomorrow I'll ask someone to marry me. The first one I meet, I'll ask her. Then I'll live a lie for the rest of my life or until I win Vivi DeVille. She is like a part of me. I can't imagine living without her. I'm going to buy a mansion. She'll be impressed. Then I'll give a party and invite everyone who's anyone, including the DeVilles."

In his tortured mind, Jean Paul conceived one evil plot after another until he settled on inviting his sister Ouida to attend the party as his fiancée. He surely wouldn't tell her the truth, for fear she didn't agree with his methods, but he had no choice.

On acquiring the home, he did invite his mother to see to the decor, and to be the hostess at his party. Ouida would arrive for the party and he would introduce her to everyone as his fiancée. That should allay Ben DeVille's fears if he had any, and give him a chance to talk to Vivi.

Although Vivi gave him no cause to think she was interested in him, his obsession with her led him to the most outlandish schemes. Remembering that he did not know enough about her, he engaged the services of W. W. Walker Detective Agency in New York. Not that it mattered to him whether there was anything sordid in her past, but if there were secrets that her husband didn't know, maybe he could let the information slip. Anything that would cause a rift between them would be welcome. He wanted her like he never wanted another woman, not only for the obvious reasons; he wanted to possess her to have her to and for himself. Luckily they had accepted his invitation, and as the day drew near, his heart throbbed with increased anticipation.

His mother saw him with another drink in hand and her heart went out to her son. If only he would give up that quest he was on and return home.

The detective agency looked into the personal life of Vivi McNeil and was taken back to her grandfather. He seemed to have been somewhat less than honest in his dealings, as it was alleged. But surely the indiscriminate nature of her grandfather, Reb McNeil, was not enough, even if they were proven to be true. Jean Paul was confident that the great Ben DeVille would not be affected by her ancestral failings. There had to be more.

Each insidious conception pushed him further from reality, and he managed to convince himself that whatever he did was all for the sake of love. His drinking was becoming a problem at the hospital, but he told them he could handle it. He intended to give it up as soon as he achieved his goal, but he found it difficult to think without it.

In his inquiries, he did hear that she was fluent in several languages; then he would have to do some more checking. On hearing she partially grew up in France, he thought that would be the place to find the real dirt. In his mind nobody could be as spotless as Vivi DeVille appeared to be. Intrigue, love and hate were all at once combined in his convoluted mind. Hate for Ben was soon enforced by envy and he became restless as he waited for a report from the detective agency.

Then, to his utter consternation, they told him the only time her name was ever connected to a man was when she was said to be in love with the great Parisian designer, Rojea Molen. And he, she found out later, was in love with his chauffeur, Jean Louis Boulet.

It also came to his knowledge that she was very wealthy, and that did a little more than pique his interest. Now he was positive Ben didn't need her as much as he.

After all, Ben was himself wealthy and could easily go back to his old life of womanizing.

He used all his liquid assets to purchase the grand old mansion overlooking the city, and it was being redone especially for him, thanks to his wonderful mother, who came early to supervise. "Vivi will be impressed," he said. His mother's heart ached for him, but there was nothing she could do.

The day Ouida was to arrive, her plane was delayed, and unfortunately, Jean Paul was on duty. Consequently, he left the airport to return later. Meanwhile, Ross Trevek was waiting for a friend of the family and literally bumped into her. "Excuse me!" he said.

"Oh, I'm sorry," she said. "It was my fault."

In that awkward moment, Ross took the initiative and said, "I'm Ross Trevek."

"Yes!" Ouida said hesitantly, "I'm Ouida Mariel."

"Are you waiting for someone special?" Ross asked.

"Oh, yes. My brother, Dr. Jean Paul Mariel. Do you know him?"

"Sure, and if he doesn't come on time, it would be my pleasure to take you home."

"Well, I wouldn't want Jean Paul to come here and find that I've gone."

"I understand," Ross said and turned to leave.

"Oh, wait!" she said. "Maybe I could call the hospital and tell him I'm on my way, assuming he hasn't left already."

"That's a good idea."

Ouida located a telephone and called the hospital, hoping her brother was still there, and so he was. She left a message to tell him she was on her way, and went back to call Ross. There was something about him that attracted her to him. He looked to be about six two, he was lean and burnished — almost bronze like — and she wondered what he did for a living, seeing he was so muscular. He appeared at her side and she said, "My brother will wait for me at the hospital, that is, if you're still offering to take me there."

"Sure!" said Ross. "It's on my way. I'd be delighted to take you there." His party arrived and all three of them loaded into the Land Rover. Ross was almost intoxicated by her presence as she sat beside him, and her perfume wafted through the evening breeze like a delicate, unknown flower. They said very little to each other, but for Ross, just being there with her was enough. He could have driven a shorter route, but he went around in order to drop off the friend first.

On their way to the hospital he said, "Ouida. That's a lovely name."

"Thank you," she said.

"How long will you be here?"

"That I can't say. As long as my brother needs me, I guess."

"One more question," said Ross. "What will you go back to when you do leave?"

"College."

"Okay, here we are." He opened the door for her, got her bags and took her to the information desk.

"Hello!" she said to the girl sitting at the desk. "Would you please page Dr. Mariel?"

"Yes, of course." Then she continued, "Are you his fiancée? He's been worried sick about not knowing if you were coming. Paging Dr. Mariel!" was all Ross heard as he escaped through the double doors.

Ouida wasn't sure what happened, but she never even had a chance to thank him. Oh, dear! she thought. He thinks I lied to him. I'll have to get used to this deception I allowed Jean Paul to talk me into. But there can't be two of him on this island. I'll find him.

Ross was miserable as he drove home. He could still feel her sitting there beside him. To think he hadn't even touched her except when they collided at the airport, but there was something remarkably different about her. Only, why would she lie about being Jean Paul Mariel's sister? On reaching home, he parked the Land Rover, wound up the windows and sat quietly lost in thought. He was playing over and over the scene at the hospital and realized it did take place. There was no misunderstanding on his part.

Ben's voice broke through to his consciousness, and he got out and joined him in the parlor. "Hey, man!" said Ben. "You look like you've seen a ghost. What happened?"

Ross related his encounter with this wonderful stranger, and Ben began to laugh, almost uncontrollably. When he regained his composure, he said, "In the words of my cousin Marguerite, I think 'the Mademoiselle Cupid has smiled on you.'"

"What are you talking about, Ben? I don't even know this girl!"

"Yes, but if you could see the look on your face as you describe her, or hear the way you say her name, you would agree. I tell you, you're in love!"

"A lot of good that will do me. She told me whenever she was finished here, she was going back to college."

"Finish what?" asked Ben.

"I don't know. Her exact words were, 'When my brother doesn't need me anymore.'"

"And you said the receptionist called her his fiancée? Hmmm," said Ben. "It sounds like there's a proverbial 'fly in the ointment.' One of them is lying, and I do believe it's the good doctor. Anyway, we'll all be attending his Christmas party, so we'll find out then."

"Ben, that's almost three weeks away. Do you expect me to wait that long?"

By this time, Ben was doing all he could not to begin laughing again. "We'll get to the bottom of this. I promise, Ross. Now go to bed and try to sleep," he said over his shoulder, expecting Ross to throw something at him.

However, for some unexplained reason, Ben was unable to sleep that night. He couldn't get Ross's story out of his mind. It was obvious that Dr. Jean Paul Mariel was planning something strange. But what could it be?

When the invitation to the party came, Ben was glad to get Vivi to do a bit of socializing for the holidays. He wanted her to believe that was all they would be doing. Then when she least expected, he would give her his surprise. The reservation was all made for them to celebrate New Year's Eve at the Waldorf Astoria in New York. She would find it in her gift on Christmas morning. He couldn't wait to see her reaction.

In the meantime, Ross was dealing with his restlessness. He decided he'd go out wih the fishermen that night, since he wasn't able to sleep. He drove over to the pier and waited for the men, who were very happy to have him aboard. They all worked for him, but one never would have known it by seeing them together. He supplied some of the hotels and restaurants, even the hospitals. Everything was done on a wholesale basis, and he had a cold storage in which was kept a certain quantity at all times. Therefore, the men fished constantly. Ross always thought it fun to be out on the ocean. It was like escaping whatever was on land. Only on this occasion, he couldn't get rid of what was ailing him. Who was Ouida? And how would he see her again?

Ross came ashore with a new resolve. He would find Ouida and get the truth from her, instead of driving himself crazy. The engine of his Thunderbird hummed as he sped toward the hospital. He had no intention of going in, but if anybody knew what was going on, it would be that receptionist.

He waited in the car until he saw a goup of boys hanging around, and called one of them. "What's your name?"

"James, sir."

"How would you like to earn this?" He waved a twenty at him.

"Really, sir?" the boy said excitedly. "What would I have to do?"

Ross quickly gave him instructions, and ten minutes later the boy was back with the information. Ross gave him the bill and raced away. He went back home and took

Ben's boat, which he had renamed *Incognito*, and cruised down the bay until he reached the beach area.

Ouida lay on the beach, but her mind was on the man she had met the night before. From his rugged look, he could have been a lifeguard, but somehow there seemed to be more to him. Where was he? She looked in all the places around the area, but he was nowhere to be found.

Ross took a few guys with him, and after they dropped anchor, he and one of them went ashore. They walked the beach casually, or so one would think, with eyes for only one face.

Suddenly there she was, alone, as beautiful as he remembered, lost in thought. "Hello," he said.

She looked startled. "Where did you come from?" she said.

"Over there!" he said, pointing to the boat.

"Oh?" she said in mock surprise.

"You have permission to come aboard."

"From whom?" she said.

"From me."

"How safe would I be on board?"

"It's pretty sturdy. It won't sink, if that's what you're worried about."

She laughed. "Are you in the habit of hearing only what you want to hear, Ross?"

"I try. Now, are you free to go with us?"

"I guess I'll take my chances. After last night, I do owe you an explanation."

"Can it wait until we get aboard?"

"Sure," she said. Somehow she wanted him to know that she hadn't lied to him.

"Now," said Ross. "What would you like to tell me?"

"The same thing I told you last night. I am Ouida Mariel. Jean Paul is my brother, but he said he wanted me to act as his fiancée to get at some girl named DeVille. Do you know their family?"

"Yes. What else did he tell you about her?"

"Not much, except he's acting so crazy over her, I can't wait to meet her. I hate to pretend, but I promised him I would, so you mustn't breathe a word to anyone."

"Does that mean it's okay for us to see each other?"

"Yes," she said, "but it has to be our secret."

"Fine with me. I'm so relieved, Ouida. I thought you were really his fiancée and I panicked. That's why I came looking for you. But there's something I must tell you. Ben DeVille is my brother, and the girl your brother mentioned is his wife. They met while she was a patient in the hospital, but I would risk my neck and swear she didn't encourage him. She's not like that. She wouldn't leave Ben for anything. They're happy together. Why would he want to cause them trouble? Vivi is like a sister to me, and I'll do whatever it takes to protect her and my brother."

"I'm sorry, Ross, but he never told me she was married. But he's acting so strange, I think he's a bit over the edge. I apologize for his behavior, Ross, and I promise I'll see that no one gets hurt."

"Thanks, but can we join forces? We could be like a form of secret service, you know?"

"Yes," she said as she searched his eyes for the evidence she needed.

That was the beginning of a wonderful, though secret, romance. They spent most of their waking hours together, as Ross showed her the island by sea as well as land. Then all too soon, it was Christmas Eve and time for the party.

Chapter Thirteen

The road to the "top hill" mansion was winding, circling the hill to form a kind of pyramid. From the peak, one could see the entire city below, and with flickering lights everywhere, the view was simply breathtaking. Mariel's sense of anticipation grew as the guests began to arrive. It was all so grand, he thought, but in his excitement he spent a lot of time at the bar.

His mother was a superb hostess with Ouida by her side, while he waited for his big moment. There were by then a hundred and fifty people present when he said, a little too loudly, "May I have your attention, please! I thank you all for coming, and may I present to you the beautiful Ouida Adiere, my fiancée." The shock on his mother's face was noticed by only a few people as the rest cheered and congratulated him.

When Ross arrived, she welcomed him warmly, and when they danced later on, there was noticeable intimacy between them. Jean Paul was seething with anger. "What are you trying to do to me?" he screamed at his sister. "You promised to help me!"

Everyone who heard his shouts thought he was jealous of the attention Ouida, his supposed fiancée, was paying to Ross. But he could feel that he was losing the battle, and obviously she was falling for the brother of his enemy. "Is that where you've been spending your time away from home?" he asked.

"Yes!" Ouida said, and left him standing there in disbelief.

Just then, Vivi and Ben walked in. She looked even more beautiful than he remembered, and his lust for her grew as he watched her in dismay. What if he had gone through all that expensive deception for nothing? Could it be that his own sister betrayed him?

Ouida had wandered up to the roof, only to find Ross was already there. The night air was fragrant with scents from land and sea, and the stars seemed to have a radiant glow. "What are you thinking about, Ouida?" Ross said, holding her to himself from behind.

"I'm just making a wish," she said.

"And so am I."

"What is your wish, Ross?"

"I wish you would consent to marry me."

"Did you ask me?"

"No, but I am now."

"I need time to think."

"How much time?"

"Two more minutes – yes."

"Merry Christmas," Ross said, taking from his inner pocket an engagement ring like none she had ever seen.

"I love you, Ross, but you do understand this has to be kept a secret until my brother gets help."

"I can wait, but now let's rejoin the party before we're missed."

On entering the foyer, they saw Ben and Vivi. Ross was beaming. "Ouida, this is Ben and Vivi, my brother and sister-in-law."

Ouida took one look at Ben and Vivi as a couple and sympathized with her brother. She was beautiful, but seemed so unaffected by it. Ben was handsome and built like an athlete. They were a great couple.

Jean Paul Mariel watched from the hall, waiting for the moment, and as soon as it came, he took it. "Mademoiselle DeVille," he said with outstretched arms, "may I have this dance?"

Ben winked at her and she said, "Sure."

"How have you been?" he said as he danced.

"Fine," replied Vivi.

"How is he treating you, I mean."

"Are you referring to my husband, Doctor? We're very happy. That little incident has been just a misunderstanding. I hear you're engaged! Best of luck to you. I hope you'll both be as happy as we are."

The music stopped and Vivi smiled at him and took her leave. Ben was waiting for her with a silly grin on his face. "You're so sure of yourself, Ben DeVille, but then, you have reason to be. You are the only man for me, and you know it."

Meanwhile, Nurse Wiley wasn't sure whom she hated more, Jean Paul Mariel or Vivi DeVille. Before she came, Jean Paul was very close to asking her to marry him. He was really beginning to see how much she loved and needed him. But now he spent every waking moment brooding over Vivi DeVille. If she didn't want him for herself, she would surely enjoy watching Ben DeVille getting a taste of his own medicine. From where she stood, she could see Jean Paul talking to a man whom she didn't recognize. She slowly worked her way over to them and said, "Hi! This is a nice place you've got here."

"Thank you!" he slurred. Then, looking at the other man, he said, "This is Nurse Wiley, and this is Sam."

The stranger answered, "My pleasure."

Neither of the two spoke again and she knew she was dismissed. They were still standing there while she silently wended her way toward the door, looking at the people who didn't even notice she was present. What an arrogant bunch, she thought. Why did I even bother to come? And yet she knew why: she loved him.

From somewhere in the shadows, Dr. Grey was watching Ben and Vivi DeVille as they talked animatedly, completely absorbed in each other. He envied them, but he was happy too. Especially for her. She deserved to be happy. When Dr. Mariel invited him, he had declined, but after he told him the purpose for the party, he knew he had to go. He couldn't allow her to be hurt again. Misery in one's life should not be perpetuated. This time she would be free to live her life, the kind she really deserved. Somehow in his failing, vermiculated mind, Vivi was not herself. To him she was Jeanette DeVille, the only woman he had really loved.

However, when he arrived, he realized he couldn't do it. He was a physician, not a murderer. What was he going to do to save her? His head ached as he resigned himself to helplessness, knowing all he could do was wait. For, as much as he could tell from watching the good doctor, he thought he was bound to drink himself to death anyway. Abruptly, he turned and left the way he came.

Ouida and Ross were dancing along with several other couples when there was a sudden crash in the dining room. Dr. Jean Paul Mariel was lying on the floor, unconscious. "Someone get a doctor!" a woman shouted.

Nurse Wiley rushed to his side. "What happened?" she said. "I'm a nurse."

"He simply fell," said an older gentleman on the other side of the room.

Nurse Wiley took charge. She cleared the area, but when she checked his vital signs, she simply sat down, rested his head on her lap first, then cradled him in her arms and began to hum. She had seen enough corpses to know there was nothing anyone could do for him professionally. But mentally, she couldn't cope with the loss. She just sat there rocking and humming a lullaby to the corpse in her arms.

His mother rushed in. "Oh, what have you done? Ouida! Where is Ouida?" she cried. "Come quick, it's your brother. I think he's dead."

The guests stood around wide-eyed and confused. Ouida appeared with Ross by her side.

"Her brother?" said one woman to her husband.

Not able to hold out any longer, his mother broke down and said, "I'm sorry, but this is my daughter. Her brother asked her to pose as his fiancée to make someone jealous. I was against it from the start, but he was my son. What could I do?"

"Who was this woman?" asked a policeman who had just arrived.

"He never said," replied his mother, "but he was so obsessed with her that if he thought his plan had failed, no one knows what he might have done."

Ouida took her mother from the room and tried unsuccessfully to console her. Later, she was given a sedative and she finally fell asleep.

It had to be his heart, Ouida thought, but there were also other possibilities. However, the coroner's report should explain the cause of death. Why speculate? Jean Paul was so young and healthy. He drank too much, but he was her brother. Yes, he was covetous, envious, hateful, greedy and deceitful, but what would she do without him? She never even had the chance to tell him about her love for Ross. He was so consumed by his hate. When did he change into such a monster?

When the autopsy was performed on Dr. Jean Paul Mariel's body, there was no indication of foul play. His heart had simply stopped. Ouida knew a heart attack could be induced, but she accepted the coroner's decision. After all, even if her suspicions were founded, whom would she accuse? She would miss him so much, and she knew her mother was devastated by his death. However, they both would have to go on with their lives.

She told her mother of her engagement to Ross and she was genuinely delighted. It was good to have him around also for support. It was agreed that after their marriage, they would occupy the mansion and allow their mother to return home.

Ben and Vivi DeVille flew to New York on December 30th to celebrate the coming of the New Year. The Waldorf Astoria was crowded as usual, and they met Marguerite and her fiancée, Romere, who were staying at the Fifth Avenue apartment for the holidays. They all joined in the festivities and toasted everyone for a happy new year. When they offered Vivi champagne, she refused. Instead, she had bitter lemon on ice.

"Aren't you feeling well?" asked someone at their table with a hint of alarm in her voice.

"I'm fine," she said. "Can't be any better, but I want to start the new year soberly. No more 'galavantin" as dear Annie would say, and definitely no alcohol."

Ben looked at her curiously, but decided not to belabor the point. He didn't dare bring up the subject that entered his thoughts. He could only hope. But by the time they got to their suite, Vivi was bursting with joy. She just couldn't keep it any longer. "Happy new year, Ben," she said. "I can't stand it any longer. I'm pregnant. I've suspected for a while, but I wanted to be sure so as not to disappoint you again. I promise to take all the necessary precautions. I'm even going to see a pediatrician here before we leave for home."

"My dear Vivi, I love you so much." He picked her up and kissed her. "You have given me the best New Year's gift any man could ever hope for."

Seven months later, Vivi gave birth to identical twin girls. Ben was overjoyed. "What am I going to do with three beautiful girls?" he quipped.

"Well," said Vivi in repartee," I'm sure you'll think of something."

Vivi had achieved what most women only dream of. She was loved as completely as she had loved. Now, with her husband and children, she was positive she was the happiest woman in the world.

Effortlessly, Vivi DeVille dazzled the people whose lives she touched, with her guileless spirit and concern for the individual. She was a natural woman, who never sought for evil, but believed in and cherished the good which she knew was somehow in all people. With the help of her husband, she successfully launched the orphanage which was one of her dreams. She also completed her cookbook which she called *Nourriture Exotique.* But to her, the essence of her accomplishment was "love" — love for her husband, her children and the purity of her life. As time passed, she had two sons and another daughter, and she realized the wait was worth it all. She vowed to encourage her three precious daughters to keep themselves pure, which is the source of their strength as women. For herself, if she had it to do over again, she wouldn't change a thing.

Yes, life was good, and at age twenty-nine, there was always the possibility of some exciting project in the future. However, at the moment, she would concentrate on publishing her book and enjoying her family, which in her mind was her contribution to the celebration of love, and life.

About the Author

Born and educated in Jamaica, West Indies, D. Iona Williams emigrated to the United States in 1968, settled in New York and later became a citizen.

In continued pursuit of a writing career, she attended New York University in the fall of 1987, where she did an independent study of fiction writing.

She enjoys writing on various subjects; however, most of her work is yet to be seen.

A mother of two grown children and three grandchildren, she now resides in Florida, where she continues to write.

This is her first publication.